"Sometimes," he said

Cole's hand was warm, strong. He didn't immediately let her go, and a strange feeling surged up her arm, pushing into her chest.

Time seemed to stop. She stood still and drank in his appearance. He was such a gorgeous, sexy man. His smoke-gray eyes were dark with emotion. She noticed once again that his shoulders were broad, arms toned, chest defined. He seemed to radiate a power that was more than just physical.

She fought another urge to go to him. It couldn't happen...not this time.

* * *

The Missing Heir
is part of the #1 bestselling miniseries
from Harlequin Desire—
Billionaires and Babies:
Powerful men...
wrapped around their babies' little fingers.

* * *

If you're on Twitter,
tell us what you think of Harlequin Desire!
#harlequindesire

Dear Reader,

While living in the far north, I've had extraordinary opportunities to discover the lifestyles and philosophies of people who build their lives in Alaska. Their independence and sense of adventure is both impressive and awe-inspiring.

In *The Missing Heir*, Alaskan bush pilot Cole Henderson is compelled to make an anonymous, whirlwind trip to Atlanta to protect the interests of his newly orphaned baby half brother, Zachary. The Atlanta Henderson clan knows nothing of Cole's existence, and he's content to keep it that way. But when feisty, beautiful Amber Welsley steps between Zachary and the warring factions bent on controlling the family's billion-dollar airline, Cole knows he has to stay and watch her back. Trouble is, he loves what he sees, and soon the last thing he wants to do is leave.

I hope you enjoy a glimpse of Alaska in *The Missing Heir*.

Happy reading!

Barbara Dunlop

THE MISSING HEIR

—

BARBARA DUNLOP

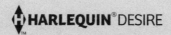

HARLEQUIN®DESIRE

Recycling programs
for this product may
not exist in your area.

ISBN-13: 978-0-373-73356-9

The Missing Heir

Printed in U.S.A.

Books by Barbara Dunlop

Harlequin Desire

Silhouette Desire

*Montana Millionaires: The Ryders
ΔColorado Cattle Barons

Other titles by this author available in ebook format.

BARBARA DUNLOP

writes romantic stories while curled up in a log cabin in Canada's far north, where bears outnumber people and it snows six months of the year. Fortunately she has a brawny husband and two teenage children to haul firewood and clear the driveway while she sips cocoa and muses about her upcoming chapters. Barbara loves to hear from readers. You can contact her through her website, www.barbaradunlop.com.

For Mom

One

Cole Henderson propped himself against a workbench in Aviation 58's hangar at the Juneau, Alaska, airport and gazed at the front page of the Daily Bureau. He realized news of the Atlanta plane crash deaths should make him feel something. After all, Samuel Henderson had been his biological father. But he had no idea what he was supposed to feel.

A nearby door in the big building opened, letting in a swirl of frigid air and blowing snow. At ten o'clock in the morning, it was still dark outside this far north.

His business partner, Luca Dodd, strode in, crossing the concrete floor alongside the sixty-passenger Komodor airplane that was down for maintenance.

"You looking at it?" Luca asked.

"I'm looking at it," said Cole.

Luca tugged off his leather gloves and removed his wool hat. "What do you think?"

"I don't think anything." Cole folded the paper and tossed it on the bench behind him. "What's to think? The guy's dead."

A drill buzzed on the far side of the hangar, and the air compressor started up, clattering in the background as two maintenance engineers worked on the engine of the Komodor.

"He was your father," Luca pointed out.

"I never met him. And he never even knew I existed."

"Still…"

Cole shrugged. His mother Lauren's marriage to billionaire Samuel Henderson, whose family owned Atlanta-based Coast Eagle Airlines, had been short-lived and heartbreaking for her. She'd never hidden Cole's heritage from him, but she'd certainly warned him about the Henderson family.

"Eight dead," said Luca, spinning the paper so the headline was right side up.

"Sounds like it all went to hell in the final seconds." As a pilot, Cole empathized with in-air emergencies. He knew the pilots would have been fighting to safely land the airplane until the very end.

"Early speculation is a combination of icing and wind shear. That's freakishly rare for Atlanta."

"We all know how bad that can go."

"An Alaskan pilot might have helped," said Luca.

Cole didn't argue that point. Pilots in Alaska had more experience than most in icy conditions.

He glanced over his shoulder at the headline once again. On a human level, he felt enormous sympathy for those who'd lost their lives, and his heart went out to their friends and family who had to go on without them. But for him personally, Samuel Henderson was nothing but a stranger who'd devastated his mother's life thirty-two years ago.

By contrast, when his mother, Lauren, had passed away from cancer last year, Cole had mourned her deeply. He still missed her.

"They put up a picture of the baby on the website," said Luca.

The article had mentioned that Samuel and his beautiful young wife, Coco, had a nine-month-old son, who, luckily, hadn't accompanied them on the trip. But Samuel's aging mother and several company executives had been on board when the family jet had crashed into the Atlanta runway.

"Cute kid," Luca added.

Cole didn't answer. He hadn't seen the picture, and he had no plans to look at it. He wasn't about to engage in the Henderson tragedy on any level.

Luca leaned forward, putting his face closer to Cole's. "You do get it, right?"

"What's to get?" Cole took a sideways step and started walking toward a hallway that led to the airline's offices. November might be Aviation 58's quietest month, but there was still plenty of work to do.

Luca walked beside him. "The kid, Zachary, is the sole survivor of that entire family."

"I'm sure he'll be well cared for." For the first time, Cole felt an emotional reaction. He wasn't proud, but it was resentment.

Immediately after their secret marriage in Vegas, Samuel had succumbed to his parents' pressure to divorce Lauren. As a young woman, she'd walked away, newly pregnant. With only a few thousand dollars to her name, she'd boarded a plane for Alaska, terrified that the powerful family would find out about her baby and take him away from her.

Hidden in Alaska, she'd scraped and saved when Cole was young. Then he'd worked night and day to put himself through flight school and to build his own airline. Zachary, by contrast, would have an army of nannies and protectors to ensure he had everything a little boy could need—from chauffeurs to private schools and ski vacations in Switzerland.

"He's all alone in the world." Luca interrupted Cole's thoughts.

"Hardly," Cole scoffed.

"You're his only living relative."

"I'm not his relative."

"You're his half brother."

"That's just an accident of genetics." There was nothing at all tying Cole to Zachary. Their lives were worlds apart.

"He's only nine months old."

Cole kept on walking across the cavernous hangar.

"If the Hendersons are as bad as Lauren said they were..." Luca's voice trailed off again, leaving the bangs and shouts of the maintenance crew to fill in the silence.

Cole picked up his pace. "Those Hendersons are all dead."

"Except for you and Zachary."

"I'm not a Henderson."

"You looked at your driver's license lately?"

Cole tugged the heavy hallway door open. "You know what I mean."

"I know exactly what you mean. The jackals in Atlanta might very well be circling an innocent baby, but you'd rather walk away from all this."

"I don't *have* to walk away from this. I was never involved in it to begin with."

Cole's operations manager, Carol Runions, poked her head out of her office. "One seventy-two has gone mechanical."

Cole glanced at his watch. Flight 172, a ninety-passenger commuter jet, was due to take off for Seattle in twenty minutes. "Is maintenance on board?" he asked Carol.

"They're on their way out there now. You want me to prep Five Bravo Sierra?"

"What's the problem?" Luca asked her.

"Indicator light for cabin pressure."

"Probably a faulty switch," said Cole. "But let's warm up Five Bravo Sierra."

"You got it," said Carol, heading back into her office.

"If we take the Citation, we can be there in four hours," said Luca.

Cole stared at his partner in confusion. "There are ninety passengers on 172." The Citation seated nine.

"I meant you and me."

"Why would we go to Seattle?" And why did Luca think it would take them four hours to get there?

"Atlanta," said Luca.

Cole's jaw went lax.

"You gotta do it," said Luca.

No, he didn't. And Cole was done with talking about the Henderson family. Without answering, he turned to walk away, shaking his head as he went.

"You gotta do it," Luca called after him. "You know as well as I do, the jackals are already circling."

"Not my problem," Cole called back.

The Atlanta Hendersons had gotten along perfectly well without him up to now. He had no doubt their *i*'s were dotted and *t*'s crossed for every possible life or death contingency. They didn't need him, and he didn't want them.

Amber Welsley folded her hands on the top of the massive inlaid-maple table in the formal dining room of the Henderson family mansion. She was one of a dozen people riveted on Max Cutter at the table's head. Max's suit was well cut, his gray hair neatly trimmed and his weathered expression was completely inscrutable as he drew a stack of papers from his leather briefcase.

From the finely upholstered chair next to hers, Amber's friend Destiny Frost leaned in close. "Six lawyers in the same room. This is not going to end well."

"Seven lawyers," Amber whispered back.

Destiny's glance darted around. "Who'd I miss?"

"You. You're a lawyer."

"Yeah, but I'm the good guy."

Amber couldn't help flexing a tiny smile. She appreciated the small break in the tension.

Max was about to read Samuel Henderson's last will and testament. The others gathered in the room had an enormous amount at stake—about a billion dollars and control of Coast Eagle Airlines. But the only thing that mattered to Amber was Zachary. She hoped whatever arrangements Samuel and her stepsister, Coco, had made for the baby's guardianship would allow Amber to stay a part of his life.

Amber was ten years older than Coco, and the two had never been close. But Amber had been instrumental in her stepsister meeting Samuel at a Coast Eagle corporate function two years ago, and Coco's pregnancy had brought them closer together for a short time. Since then, Amber had felt a special kinship with Zachary.

Across the wide table from her, vice president of operations Roth Calvin shifted in his seat. Since the day the company's president, Dryden Dunsmore, had been killed in the plane crash, the three vice presidents had been running the show. Now Samuel's will would reveal who would get control of Coast Eagle.

Whoever it was would control Roth Calvin's future. Much further down the corporate ladder, as assistant director of finance, Amber didn't much care who took over the helm of the company. Her day-to-day job as an accountant wasn't about to change.

"My personal apologies for the delay in scheduling this reading," Max opened, his gaze going around the room. "But there were several complexities to this case due to the number of deaths involved."

Amber's throat thickened. She quickly swallowed to combat the sensation. Poor Coco had only been twenty-one.

"I'll start with Jackie Henderson's will," said Max. "I'll follow that with her son, Samuel's, which was written jointly with his wife, Coco. In addition, there is a small codicil, executed by Coco alone. I would caution you all to draw no conclusions until I've finished reading all three."

Max straightened the papers. "Aside from some small bequests to friends and long-time staff members, and a generous donation of ten million dollars to the Atlanta arts community, Jackie Henderson has left her estate to her son, Samuel, including her twenty-five percent ownership of Coast Eagle Airlines."

Nobody in the room reacted to Max's statements, and they gave only a cursory glance to the list of bequests handed around. That Samuel was Mrs. Henderson's heir was completely expected. And though Mrs. Henderson had been an exacting and irritable old woman, she had long been a patron of the arts.

"As to the last will and testament of Samuel Henderson…" said Max.

Everyone stilled in their seats.

Max looked down at a page in front of him. "Mr. Henderson has also left a list of small, specific bequests, and has made several charitable donations, also ten million dollars to the Atlanta arts community, along with an additional ten million dollar scholarship to the Georgia Pilots Association."

Max took a sip of water. "As to the bulk of Mr. Henderson's estate, I'll read directly from the document. 'My entire estate is left in trust, in equal shares, to my legitimate children. So long as my wife, Coco Henderson, remains guardian of my children, and until they reach the age of majority, business decisions pertaining to the children's interest in Coast Eagle Airlines will be made by Dryden Dunsmore.'"

There was a collective intake of breath in the room, followed by murmured sidebar conversations.

"Well, there's a complexity," Destiny whispered to Amber.

It was obvious Samuel had not contemplated Dryden Dunsmore dying along with him.

Max cleared his throat, and everyone fell silent.

"'Should my wife predecease me,'" he continued, "'guardianship of my minor children will go to Roth Calvin.'"

The room went completely silent, and a dozen gazes swung to Roth. He held his composure for a full ten seconds, but then an uncontrollable smile curved his thin lips, gratification glowing in the depths of his pale blue eyes.

A buzz of conversation came up in the room.

Roth turned to the lawyer on his right. His tone was low, but Amber heard every word. "With Dryden out of the picture, do I have control over the shares?"

The lawyer nodded.

Roth's smile grew wider and more calculating.

"The codicil," Max interrupted the various discussions.

People quieted down again, and Roth's expression settled into self-satisfaction.

"To give some context to this…" said Max. "And I do apologize for being so direct on such an emotional matter. Samuel Henderson was pronounced dead at the accident scene, while Coco Henderson was pronounced dead during the ambulance ride to the hospital."

Amber's stomach tightened. She'd been assured Coco had not regained consciousness after the crash, but she couldn't help but be reminded of the fear and horror her stepsister must have experienced in those final seconds while the plane attempted to land in the storm.

"As such, Samuel is deemed to have predeceased his wife." Max held a single sheet of paper. "Given that fact, Coco Henderson's codicil is legal and valid. It modifies the joint will in only one way." He read, "'I leave guardianship of my child or children to my stepsister, Amber Welsley.'"

Amber could feel shock permeate the room. Jaws literally dropped open and gazes swung to her. Roth's glare sent a wave of animosity that nearly pushed her backward.

Beneath the table, Destiny grasped her hand.

"What about business decisions?" Roth barked. "That woman is in no position to run the company. She's an assistant."

"Assistant *director,*" Destiny corrected.

Amber was in a management position, not a clerical one.

Roth sneered at them both. "Samuel clearly wanted someone qualified in charge of business decisions on behalf of his son."

"It's a valid question," said Max. "For the moment, Amber Welsley has guardianship over Zachary, including all rights and responsibilities to manage and safeguard his ownership position in Coast Eagle."

"But—" Roth began.

Max held up a hand to forestall him. "For any changes to that, you'll need a decision from a judge."

"You can bet we're going to a judge," spat Roth.

Amber whispered to Destiny, "What does this all mean?"

"It means we're going to court to duke it out with Roth. And it means he just became your mortal enemy. But right now, it also means you get Zachary."

Amber's chest swelled tight. Zachary would stay with her. For now, nothing else mattered.

Walking through the entrance of the Atlanta hotel ballroom, Cole gazed at the crowds of people attending the Georgia Pilots Association annual fund-raiser. Tonight was the formal recognition of the new Samuel Henderson Memorial Scholarship, so he knew the who's who of Coast Eagle Airlines would be in the room.

Luca was beside him, dressed in a formal suit. "You'll be glad you came."

"I'll mostly be glad if it shuts you up."

Cole had told himself a thousand times that the Hendersons of Atlanta were none of his business, and he still believed it. But Luca had kept after him for three long weeks. Finally, Cole had given in and checked out a picture of Zachary on a news site.

The baby was cuter than he'd expected, and his face had seemed strangely familiar. But Cole chalked it up to the power of suggestion. When you started looking for a family resemblance, everything took on new meaning. Sometimes gray eyes were simply gray eyes.

But once he'd scratched the surface, he'd ended up reading the rest of the article, learning there was a court challenge for guardianship. He didn't necessarily agree with Luca that everyone involved was a jackal out to get the kid's money. But he did find himself analyzing the players.

In the end, his curiosity won out, and he agreed to make the trip to Atlanta. He had no intention of marching up to the front door and introducing himself as a long-lost relative. He was staying under the radar, checking things out and returning to Alaska just as soon as he confirmed Zachary was safe.

"Right there," said Luca. "In the black dress, lace sleeves, brown hair, kind of swooped up. She's at the table below the podium. She's moving right now."

As Cole zeroed in on Amber Welsley, she turned, presenting him with a surprisingly pretty profile.

Her diamond jewelry flashed beneath the bright lights, accenting her feminine face. Her dress was classic, a scooped neckline, three-quarter-length lace sleeves that blended to a form-fitting bodice and a narrow skirt that emphasized her trim figure.

From this distance, she surprised him. She wasn't at all what he'd expected. She was younger, softer, insidiously captivating. While he stared at her, the wholly inappropriate thought that she was kissable welled up in his mind.

"You want to go over and say hi?" asked Luca.

The true answer was no. Cole wanted to get on an airplane and fly back to Alaska.

He might as well get this over with. Checking out Amber and all the other characters in this family drama was his purpose in being here. There wasn't any point waiting.

"Let's do it," he said.

"Roth Calvin's at the next table," said Luca as they walked. "He's facing us, talking to the guy with red hair, in the steel-gray jacket."

"I think you missed your calling as a spy."

Luca grinned. "I'm calling dibs on the one named Destiny."

"Who's Destiny?"

"She was in a couple of the photos with Amber Welsley. She's hot. And with a name like that, I'm definitely giving her a shot."

Cole shook his head. "She's all yours, buddy. I just want to make sure the kid's okay." Then any duty he might have as a blood relative would be done.

"By kid, you mean your baby brother?"

"Yeah, that's not a phrase we'll be using."

"Boggles the mind, doesn't it?"

"You're going to have to be boggled all by yourself. I won't be here long enough."

"You want a wingman for the intro?"

"Sure. But don't use the name Henderson."

"Undercover. I like it."

"I'll use Cole Parker. My middle name."

"Right behind you, Cole Parker."

The closer they drew to the Coast Eagle tables, the more beautiful Amber became. Her hair wasn't brown, but a rich chestnut with highlights that shimmered under the bright stage lights. It was half up, half down in a tousled bundle with wisps flowing over her temples and down her back. The scalloped neckline of her dress showed off an expanse of creamy skin, while the lace across her shoulders played peekaboo with his imagination.

Her eyes were deep blue, fringed with dark lashes. Her full lips were dark red, her cheeks enticingly flushed. He had a sudden vision of her clambering naked into his bed.

She turned as he approached, caught his stare and gave him an obviously practiced smile. He realized hundreds if not thousands of people must have introduced themselves and offered their condolences in the past weeks.

"Amber Welsley?" he asked her, offering his hand.

"I am."

"I'm Cole Parker from Aviation 58. My condolences on your loss."

"Thank you, Mr. Parker." She shook his hand.

The soft warmth of her palm seemed to whisper through his skin. He felt a ripple of awareness move up his arm and along the length of his body. Her expression flinched, and for a second he thought she'd felt it, too. But then her formal smile was back in place, and she was moving on.

Cole quickly spoke again to keep her attention. "This is my business partner, Luca Dodd."

"Please call me Luca."

"And I'm Cole," Cole put in, feeling like an idiot for not having said it right away.

"Aviation 58 was looking to contribute to the Samuel Henderson fund," said Luca.

Cole's stomach twisted, and he shot Luca a glare of annoyance.

Where had that come from? There was no way on earth Cole was contributing to something with Samuel's name on it.

"It's a very worthy cause," said Amber. But then she caught Cole's expression. "Is something wrong?"

"No," he quickly answered.

"You look upset."

"I'm fine."

She canted her head to one side, considering him. "You don't agree that the pilot scholarship is a worthy cause?"

"I believe what Luca meant is that we're thinking of setting something up in parallel. With Georgia Pilots, but not necessarily..." How exactly was he going to phrase this?

"Not necessarily in honor of Samuel Henderson?" Amber finished for him.

Cole didn't know how to respond to the direct challenge. He didn't want to lie, but he didn't want to insult her, either.

"You have a spare ten million hanging around to match Coast Eagle?" she asked.

"Ten million is a little out of our league," Cole admitted.

Her blue eyes narrowed ever so slightly. "Did you know Samuel?"

"I never met him."

The suspicious expression didn't detract at all from her beauty, and Cole experienced an urge to sweep back her hair and kiss the delicate curve of her neck.

"So you disliked him from afar?" she asked.

"I didn't…" This was getting worse by the second. Cole gave himself a mental shake. "I knew people who knew him."

"Amber?" prompted a man at her elbow.

Cole clenched his jaw at the interruption.

"Five minutes to introductions," said the man.

"Thanks, Julius." She glanced at Luca for a moment before settling her attention back on Cole. "It looks like I need to take my seat. It was a pleasure to meet you, Cole Parker."

"Are you always this polite?"

"Do you want me to be rude?"

Cole was the one who'd been rude. "This conversation didn't go the way I expected."

"Maybe you could try again some other time."

"What are you doing later?" He hadn't intended the question to sound intimate, but it did.

She didn't miss a beat. "I believe I'm eating crab cocktail and chicken Kiev, giving a short, heartfelt speech on behalf of the Henderson family, then relieving the nanny and going to sleep."

"Zachary?" Cole took advantage of the opening.

"He'll be having his bath about now. He likes splashing with the blue duck and chewing on the washcloth."

"Are you staying for the dance?"

"I doubt it."

"*Will* you stay for the dance?"

She hesitated. "You think you'll do better if we're dancing?"

"I'll try not to insult the evening's deceased honoree."

"You set a high bar."

"Underpromise and overdeliver."

The man named Julius returned, touching Amber's arm. "Amber?"

"Goodbye for now," she told Cole with a smile.

Though her expression was more polite than warm, he decided to take the words as encouraging.

"What the hell was *that?*" Luca muttered as she walked away.

"Contributing to his *scholarship?*" asked Cole. "Where did you expect me to go from there?"

"You choked."

"We are *not* contributing to his scholarship."

"You made that much clear."

They turned to wind their way between tables.

"She's not what I expected," said Cole as they returned to the back half of the big ballroom.

"She has two arms, two legs, speaks English. What did you expect?"

"I don't know." Cole struggled to organize his thoughts. "Snobbish, maybe, polished and conniving."

"She looked pretty polished to me."

"She's beautiful, but that's not the same thing."

"She's a knockout. Do you actually think she'll dance with you?"

"Why not?"

"Because you choked, and I'm sure she has other offers."

"I'm staying optimistic."

As the lights went dim and the applause came up, Cole made up his mind to approach her as soon as the dinner was over. This was by far his best chance to mingle with the Hendersons and Coast Eagle without revealing his identity, and he wanted to get it done and over with.

Two

Amber couldn't wait to get out of the ballroom. Her first choice on a Saturday night was to stay home with Zachary, tucked in her jammies with a cup of hot chocolate and an old movie. But she was the closest thing there was to a member of the Henderson family, and somebody had to graciously accept the pilots association's thanks.

Unlike her sister, Coco, Amber never attended highbrow events. Consequently, everything she wore tonight was new. Her feet were killing her in the ridiculous high heels. Her push-up bra was digging into her ribs, the lace scratching her skin. And the tight dress, chosen by Destiny, who insisted it was perfect, was restricting her movements so that she couldn't even cross her legs under the table.

The MC ended a string of thank-yous with a request for applause to compliment the catering staff. As the clapping died down, the music came up, signaling the start of the dance.

Amber breathed a sigh of relief. All that was left was to politely make her way toward the exit, find a cab and get home. She stood, tucking her tiny purse under her arm.

A fiftysomething woman she vaguely recognized grasped her hand to shake it. "Lovely speech, Ms. Welsley. Lovely speech."

"Thank you."

The woman's expression turned serious. "Even in such tragic circumstances, the Henderson family is having a positive impact on the community."

"Samuel was a very generous man," Amber responded by rote, though she had her own private thoughts on Samuel's character, most particularly his decision to marry her beautiful, impetuous, nineteen-year-old stepsister.

Amber had initially kept her distance from the couple, regretting many times the decision to bring Coco to the company party where the two had met. But then Coco had become pregnant, and Amber had been drawn back into the drama of Coco's life.

"Excuse me, Ms. Welsley," came a male voice.

The woman seemed reluctant to step back to give way.

"Good evening." Amber smiled at the new man, taking his offered hand, mentally calculating how long it would take her to run the gauntlet to the exit. It would be an hour or more at this pace. She truly didn't think she could stand that long in these shoes. For a nonsensical moment, she pictured herself toppling over onto the ballroom floor.

"I'm Kevin Mathews from Highbush Unlimited. I wonder if I might give you my card."

Amber kept her smile in place. "Certainly, Mr. Mathews."

He dug into his inside pocket for a business card. "We're a charitable organization, focused on environmental rehabilitation, primarily in the northwest. I know a lot about Mr. Henderson and Coast Eagle, and I can't help imagining that he would have been a supporter of the environmental rehabilitation."

Amber doubted that Samuel had given much thought to the environment, since he flew around in a private jet, airconditioned the heck out of his mansion and owned several gas-guzzling luxury cars.

But she took the card the man offered. "I'd be happy to pass this along to Coast Eagle's Community Outreach Unit."

His expression faltered. "If you have some time now, I could outline for you our—"

"There you are," came a deeper male voice. "I believe it's time for our dance."

Cole Parker appeared by her side, his arm held out, a broad smile on his face.

Amber couldn't tell if he was rescuing her or about to pitch something himself. But she quickly estimated that the dance floor was more than halfway to the exit. That was progress. She returned his smile and took his arm.

"Please excuse me," she said to Kevin.

Kevin's expression faltered, but he had little choice but to let her go.

Cole guided her through the crowd, keeping their pace brisk enough to discourage the people who looked as though they might approach. It was hard on her feet, particularly her baby toes, but there was no option but to keep walking. Gradually, the crowd thinned near the dance floor.

"Am I out of the frying pan and into the fire?" she asked him.

"I'm not hitting you up for a donation, if that's what you mean."

"Good to hear." She wasn't sure what he wanted, but he was persistent enough that he had to be after something.

"I brought you a gift," he told her.

"Bribery? That's a bit blatant, don't you think?"

"I believe in getting straight to the point." He lifted his palm.

She glanced down, squinting. "You bought me a pair of... socks?"

"Dancing slippers. I got them from a vending machine in the lobby." He glanced down at her black-and-gold four-inch heels. "Unless I miss my guess, those are two-hour shoes."

She grimaced. "Is that what they call them?" It was an apt name.

She knew she should be suspicious of his motives, but she couldn't help but feel grateful.

"Over here." He pointed to a couple of empty chairs at the edge of the dance floor. "Have a seat."

She eased down, deciding to accept the gift and remove the torture chambers from her feet. How much could she possibly be indebted to him for a pair of vending-machine dancing slippers?

She unbuckled the straps and slipped her feet free.

"I went with medium." He handed her the black-satin, ballet-style slippers.

Slipping them onto her feet, she nearly groaned out loud. "They're so soft."

He bent to pick up her shiny heels, dangling them from his fingertips for a moment before setting them down. "These are ridiculous."

She rose with him. "This is an important event for Coast Eagle. And Destiny says they make my calves look longer."

"Your calves are already the perfect length." He set the shoes on the chair.

"You're not even looking at them."

"I can tell by your height." He offered his arm again. "Shall we?"

"I suppose it's the least I can do, since you saved my feet. But you have to make me a promise."

"Sure."

She took his arm. "After the dance, walk me to the exit." She glanced discreetly around. "For some reason, nobody's bothering me when I'm with you."

"Were they bothering you before?"

"All evening long." She'd never experienced anything like it. "Donations, jobs and pictures. Why on earth would anybody want their picture taken with me?"

"Because you're beautiful?" He drew her into his arms.

"Ha, ha." Coco had been beautiful. Amber was, well, sensible. She was very sensible.

Not that sensible was a bad thing. And she truly didn't mind her looks. Her eyes were a pleasant shade of blue. Her nose wasn't too big. Her hair was slightly curly and had its good days and bad days. Today it had been tamed by a team of professionals, so it looked pretty good. She had to say, though, she wasn't crazy about the sticky feeling from all the products they'd used at Chez Philippe.

"I wasn't joking," said Cole.

"We both know you've got a lot of ground to make up for from earlier," she said, settling into the rhythm of the music.

"True," he agreed.

"So anything you say or do is suspect."

"You're pretty tough to compliment, you know that?"

"There's no need. I'm over the fact that you didn't like Samuel."

He paused as if weighing his next words. "You're a very good dancer."

She couldn't tell if he was mocking her or not. She'd certainly never spent much time perfecting dance steps. Was he trying to kowtow, or was he simply making small talk? Or maybe he was just getting off the topic of Samuel.

"So are you," she answered neutrally. "I can't remember where you said you were from."

"Alaska. Are you changing the subject?"

"From me to you? Yes. You're about out of things to compliment. Unless you like my hair."

"I like your hair."

"Good. It cost a lot of money to get it this way. Now back to you."

"Aviation 58 is in Juneau. The state capital. It's on the panhandle."

"You're a pilot?"

"I am. I'm also one of the owners of the airline."

"I've never heard of it."

Coast Eagle flew to Seattle and California, but they didn't venture into the north. "We're regional."

She tipped her head back to look at him. "And what brought you to Atlanta, Cole Parker?"

He gave a small shrug. "It's December. Have you seen a weather report for Alaska?"

"Not recently. Maybe never."

"It's cold up there."

"So you're on vacation?"

"For a few days, yes."

For the first time, she allowed herself to take a good look at his face. She realized he was an astonishingly handsome man, deep gray eyes, a straight nose, square chin, all topped with thick, dark hair, cut short and neat. She couldn't detect aftershave or shampoo, but there was something fresh and clean about his scent.

He was probably six-two. His shoulders were square, body fit and trim. And his big, square hands seemed strong and capable where they held her. In a flash, she realized she was attracted to him.

"Amber?" His deep voice startled her. That sound was another thing she liked about him.

"Yes?"

"I asked if there was anything in particular we should see."

Had he? How had she missed that?

She quickly corralled her thoughts. "The botanical gardens are beautiful. Or you can do outdoor ice-skating. My favorite is Atlantic Station. A little shopping, a little Christmas-light gazing, some hot chocolate." She couldn't help thinking about Zachary and the Christmas events he might enjoy as he got older.

She'd easily come to love seeing him every day. He was a bit fussy in the evenings, but the poor little guy had been through a lot. His mother and father were both gone, and he had no way of knowing why it was happening.

She was doing her best to substitute. And she'd wrapped her head around the possibility of raising a baby. Though she couldn't yet imagine her life with a child, a school-age child, then a teenager, then a young man. When she thought that far ahead, she feared she wasn't capable of pulling it off. But she knew she had to come through for him. She was all he had.

She felt a sudden urge to rush home and hold him in her arms, reassure him that she'd figure it out.

"Are we close to the exit?" she asked Cole, thinking she could slip out and get herself home.

"I'll dance you over there," said Cole. "Tired?"

"Partly. But this isn't exactly my thing."

"I thought the über-rich thrived on fresh crab, Belgian torte and champagne."

"I'm not über-rich." Though she could understand how he would make that mistake. Lately, everybody seemed to assume that guardianship of Zachary made her an instant billionaire. It was far more complicated than that.

"Right," he drawled.

She didn't want to have this debate. "Thank you for the dance, Cole."

His expression turned serious. "I did it again, didn't I? Stuffed my foot in my mouth?"

"Not at all. I am tired, and I really appreciate you escorting me across the ballroom. It was going to take hours at the rate I was going."

"I'll get you to the front doors," he offered.

"That's not necessary."

"It's my pleasure." His hand dropped to the small of her back. "I'll glower at anyone who tries to talk to us along the way."

She couldn't help but smile at that. And, to be truthful, it did seem like a prudent course of action. The lobby and foyer were full of people. Her name and face had been in the news for the past three weeks, so she was easily recognized.

"Then, thank you," she told him.

"Let's go."

He picked up the pace, drawing her across the mezzanine floor lobby and down two sets of elevators. People stared as they passed but didn't approach them. For a fleeting moment, she wondered if he'd consider a permanent gig as her escort. This was certainly more pleasant than her trek into the event.

"The doorman will get me a cab," she told Cole as they came to the glass front.

"No need. I have a car right here."

"Cole—"

"And a driver," he finished, moving through the front door. "I'm not plotting to get you alone. I'll get you home safe and sound, nothing else."

As she stepped onto the sidewalk, she felt its cold hardness through the dancing slippers, and her memory kicked in. "My shoes." She turned. "I left my shoes upstairs."

"I'll go back for them," he offered. "You don't need to walk all that way again."

"Taxi, sir?" the doorman inquired.

"I've got a car waiting," Cole answered, handing the man a tip. "A sedan for Aviation 58."

"I'll have it brought around," the doorman answered.

"I can't take your car," said Amber. How had this gotten so complicated?

"Where are you going?" asked Cole.

"Fifth Avenue and Eighty-Ninth."

"It'll only take ten minutes to get you there."

A black car pulled up in front of them and Cole opened the door.

Amber decided to go with the flow. The sooner she got going, the sooner she'd be home with Zachary. She climbed in, and Cole shut the door behind her.

But before they pulled away, he surprised her by hopping in the other side.

"I thought you were going back for my shoes."

"I'll do that after we get you home. Fifth Avenue and Eighty-Ninth," he said to the driver.

"That's ridiculous."

She couldn't understand why he'd make the round trip for nothing. Unless he was worried she'd commandeer his car for a joyride. Though she doubted the driver would let her do that.

As they pulled out of the turnaround and onto the street, she clicked through other possibilities. He'd been intensely persistent, awfully complimentary and easy to get along with, and he'd stuck to her like glue. What could he be after?

And then it came to her. The man owned an airline, a small regional West Coast airline that was likely looking to expand. She instantly realized the vacation story was a cover. Cole was here to do business.

She angled herself in the seat, facing him. "You're after our Pacific routes."

"Excuse me?"

"I figured it out. You're thinking Samuel's death makes Coast Eagle vulnerable. You're hoping we'll be looking to downsize, and you think you can get your hands on the Pacific routes to expand Aviation 58."

He stared at her for a long moment.

"You've been way too friendly," she elaborated. "You overplayed your hand."

"Maybe I'm simply attracted to you."

She gazed down at the fancy dress. She did look better than

usual, but Cole was still out of her league. "There were far more beautiful women at the event tonight."

"I didn't see them." The sincerity in his expression was quite impressive.

"Nice try. It's the routes."

"You see that as the only possible explanation?"

"I do."

"Then, I admit it. It's the routes. Will you sell them to me?"

She leaned back in the seat. "I don't know why everybody thinks I have so much power. I'm the assistant director of finance. There's still a board of directors in place, and the vice presidents are in charge of operations until they name a new president."

"But as Zachary's guardian, you control board appointments."

"Theoretically."

If she kept custody of Zachary, that would be true. But before that could ever happen, she had a big fight with Roth on her hands.

"There's nothing theoretical about it," said Cole. "The board answers to the shareholders, and the president answers to the board, and everyone else answers to the president. You can do anything you want."

"But I won't. I have my own job at Coast Eagle, and I'm not about to muscle in on anyone else's."

"It's your responsibility." There was an unexpected hardness to Cole's tone. "It's your responsibility to Zachary to take control of the company."

She turned to look at him again. "It's my responsibility to Zachary to ensure the company is well run. That doesn't mean I make any particular decision."

His dark eyes were implacable. "Yes, it does."

"Well, Mr. Cole Parker, owner of Aviation 58 in Alaska, you are certainly entitled to your opinion. And I'm more than entitled to ignore it."

He opened his mouth but then obviously thought better of speaking.

The car came to a halt at the curb.

"The Newmont Building?" the driver asked. "Or are you in Sutten's Edge?"

"This is it," said Amber, feeling anxious to get away. "Joyce Roland is the director of planning," she said to Cole. "You can ask her about the Pacific routes, but she may not take your call."

The driver had come around and now swung open her door.

"Thank you for the ride. Good night, Cole."

A small smile played on his lips. "You're very polite."

"So I've been told."

"Good night, Amber. Thank you for the dance."

A sudden rush of warmth enveloped her, and she found her gaze dropping from his eyes to his lips. For a fleeting second, she imagined him kissing her good-night.

She shook away the wayward feeling and quickly exited the car. Zachary was upstairs waiting, and Roth was in the wings with a team of high-priced lawyers. Amber didn't have time for kisses or fantasies or anything else.

Cole advanced through the hotel lobby, heading for the escalators that would take him back to the ballroom.

It didn't take him long to spot Luca coming the other way, a pretty blond woman at his side.

"There you are," said Luca as they met. "I wondered what had happened to you."

"I left something in the ballroom," said Cole.

"This is Destiny Frost. Turns out, she's a friend of Amber Welsley." Luca's expression was inscrutable.

Cole played along, pretending Luca hadn't planned to meet Destiny. "Nice to meet you." He offered his hand.

She shook, and hers was slim and cool. "It's a pleasure."

"I offered Destiny a ride home," said Luca. "You coming with us?" His expression told Cole a third wheel would not be particularly welcome.

Cole tipped his chin toward the escalator. "I have to grab something upstairs. Can you swing back and get me later?"

Luca gave a satisfied smile. "Will do."

"Luca says you're from Alaska?" asked Destiny.

"We are," Cole replied.

"I've never been there."

"It's beautiful, magnificent."

"It must be cold."

Luca stepped in. "I've already offered to keep her warm."

Destiny smiled and shook her head. "He's shameless."

"But harmless," said Cole, intending to be reassuring, but also being honest. Luca was a perfect gentleman.

"I'll text you on the way back?" asked Luca.

"Sounds good." With a nod to both of them, Cole headed for the escalator.

He was going against the crowd, most people on their way out of the event. So he easily made it to the ballroom and headed for the chair where they'd parked Amber's shoes.

To his surprise, they were gone.

"Seriously?" he muttered out loud.

He glanced around at the departing crowd. At an event this highbrow, somebody was going to steal a pair of shoes?

Then he caught a glint of gold in one of the waiter's hands. He squinted. It was definitely Amber's shoes. The man was headed toward a side exit.

Cole made a beeline after him, feeling better about human nature. The waiter obviously thought they'd been abandoned and was taking them to the hotel's lost and found.

Cole wound his way through the tables and took the same exit, coming out into a long dim hallway. One direction obviously led to the kitchen, the other down a narrow flight of stairs. It seemed unlikely that the lost and found was in the kitchen, so he took the stairs.

At the bottom, he spotted the guy about thirty yards away. He called out, and the man turned.

"The shoes," called Cole.

Before he could say anything more, the man bolted, running a few steps before shoving open a side exit.

"Are you kidding me?" Cole shouted, breaking into a run.

He burst through the side door, finding himself in an alley.

He quickly scanned the area and spotted the guy at a run. He sprinted after the man. When he caught up, he grasped the guy's left arm and spun him around, bringing him to a sliding halt.

"What's going on?" Cole gasped. "You're stealing a pair of *shoes?*"

"They're my girlfriend's." The man was gasping for breath.

"They're *my* girlfriend's." As he spoke, Cole couldn't help but take note of the man's unshaven face, and the rather wild look in his eyes. "You're not a waiter."

The man reached in his pants pocket and pulled a knife, flicking open a six-inch blade and holding it menacingly out in front of him.

"They're *shoes,*" said Cole, adrenaline rushing into his bloodstream. Admittedly, they were nice shoes. And given the Hendersons' wealth, they were likely ridiculously expensive. But what could they possibly bring this guy on the black market?

The man snarled. "Do yourself a favor and walk away."

No way was that happening. Cole was returning Amber's property to her. "Give me the shoes."

"You want to get *hurt?*"

Suddenly, a low growl sounded next to Cole. His skin prickled, and he glanced cautiously down. But the mangy dog was staring at the man with the knife. It didn't seem to be threatening Cole.

"He'll go for your throat," Cole lied.

The man glanced furtively at the dog.

The dog growled again.

"Drop the knife, or he'll attack."

The man hesitated, and the dog took a step forward. The knife clattered to the ground, along with the shoes, and the man took two rapid steps backward. Then he spun around and ran.

Cole took in the medium-size dog that was now wagging its tail, obviously feeling proud of himself.

"Good job," he told the mutt, patting its head, finding sticky, matted fur.

He looked closer and realized the animal was painfully thin.

It had a wiry, mottled coat, mostly tan, but black on the ears and muzzle. Its brown eyes looked world-weary and exhausted.

"You a stray?" Cole found himself asking.

He moved to pick up the shoes. When he straightened, the dog was watching him patiently.

"You probably want a reward for all that."

The dog blinked.

"I don't blame you." Cole blew out a breath. He supposed the least he could do was buy the animal a burger.

"Come on, then." He started down the alley toward the brightly lit street. The dog trotted at his heels.

At the front of the hotel, Cole reported the incident to one of the doormen, who sent someone to retrieve the knife. Cole learned that they'd had previous trouble with a thief impersonating a waiter at large events. If the knife had fingerprints on it, they might be able to catch the guy. It seemed likely he'd stolen more than just the shoes tonight.

Duty done, Cole and the dog then made their way down the street until they came to a fast-food restaurant.

Thinking it was a fifty-fifty shot the mutt would wait, Cole left it outside while he purchased two deluxe hamburgers. He was hungry after the fancy little portions at the pilots association event, and a burger didn't seem like the worst idea in the world.

When he returned to the street, the dog jumped to attention. It wolfed down the burger in two bites, so Cole gave it the second one, as well.

His phone chimed, and a text message told him Luca was sending back the empty car. Luca and Destiny were stopping for a nightcap.

Cole smiled at his friend's luck, tossed the wrappers in the trash and headed back toward the hotel. Predictably, the dog followed along. It was sure to be disappointed when a meal didn't appear at their next stop.

Cole took the animal back to the alley at the edge of the hotel property and pointed. "Go on, now," he told it.

It looked up at him uncomprehendingly.

"Go home," Cole commanded.

It didn't move.

He made his voice sterner. "Go on."

The dog ducked its head, eyes going sad.

Cole felt a shot to his chest.

He tried to steel himself against the guilt, but the effort didn't pay off. He crouched down in front of the dog, scratching its matted neck and meeting its eyes. "I don't know what you expect here."

It pushed forward, nuzzling its nose against Cole's thigh.

"Those are rented pants," said Cole.

It pushed farther forward.

"I live in Alaska."

Its tail began to wag.

"Crap."

"Mr. Parker?" The driver appeared in Cole's peripheral vision. "Are you ready to go, sir?"

Cole stood, drawing a deep sigh. "We're ready."

"We?"

"The dog's coming, too."

The driver glanced down at the scruffy animal. He hesitated, but then said, "Of course, sir."

"Do you have a blanket or something to protect the seat?"

"I'll get a newspaper from the doorman."

"That'll work," said Cole. He looked to the dog. "You want to go for a car ride?"

Its head lifted. Its brow went up. And its tail wagged harder.

"I'll take that as a yes." Cole knew he was making a stupid, emotional decision, one he'd likely regret very quickly. But he couldn't bring himself to leave the animal behind.

He closed his eyes for a long moment. All this for a pair of shoes.

Three

The next morning, Cole headed for the Hendersons' penthouse apartment to return Amber's shoes. He took the dog with him, thinking maybe he'd stop by the shelter on his way back and drop it off. He told himself they were in the business of finding stray animals good homes.

The dog looked much more appealing since Cole had given him a bath in the hotel's carwash bay. He smelled better, too, considerably better. And he'd probably put on five pounds between the room-service steak last night and the bacon and sausage breakfast.

The animal had been meticulously well behaved, and now stood quietly by Cole's side while Cole rang the bell.

A minute later, Amber answered the door. She was dressed in faded blue jeans, bare feet poking out at the bottom. A stained T-shirt stretched across her chest, and she had what looked like oatmeal smeared in her hair. Zachary was bawling in her arms.

"The doorman said it was a delivery," she told Cole over Zachary's cries.

Cole held up the shoes. "It is a delivery."

She focused on the shiny creations while struggling to hold the wiggling, howling Zachary. "Honestly, I'd hoped somebody might steal them."

"You have got to be kidding." Cole didn't know whether to laugh or cry.

"Only partially kidding," she admitted. "They cost a lot of money, but I don't ever want to have to wear them again." She glanced down. "You have a dog?"

"I have one now," he said.

"Okay." She seemed to digest that while Zachary continued to wriggle. It was clear she had her hands full. "Could you maybe just bring them in and toss them down?" She glanced around the foyer.

"Sure." Cole moved through the doorway, spying a closet door. He opened it and placed them inside.

The baby's cries faded to whimpers behind him.

He turned back. "I'll have you know I practically risked my life to rescue these."

Zachary suddenly stiffened. He twisted his head to stare at Cole in what looked like amazement.

"The party got that wild?" Amber asked.

Zachary's silver-gray eyes focused on Cole like lasers. He went silent and stared unblinking, seeming to drink in Cole's appearance.

Then, suddenly, he lunged for Cole.

"Hey." Amber grappled to keep hold of him.

Zachary's own arms were outstretched, reaching almost desperately for Cole. He started to howl again, hands clasping the air.

"This is weird," said Amber.

Cole didn't have a clue how to respond.

"Do you mind?" She moved closer, glancing meaningfully at the baby.

"I guess not." Who would say no?

Taking Zachary from her arms, he cautiously brought him into his chest. Zachary instantly wrapped his arms around Cole's neck, squeezing tight. He nuzzled his sticky, tear-damp face against Cole's skin. Then he sighed, and his entire body went limp against Cole's chest.

Through his shock and surprise, Cole's heart started to pound, bringing a strange tightness to his chest. For some bizarre reason, his baby brother trusted him. How was a guy supposed to react to that?

"You're magic," Amber whispered. "Whatever it is you're doing, just keep it up."

"I'm only standing here."

"He's been crying for over an hour. He gets like that sometimes."

"He probably exhausted himself before I got here."

"I think he misses his parents," Amber said softly, her expression compassionate as she gazed at Zachary. She reached out to stoke the baby's downy hair. "But he doesn't understand what he's feeling, and he certainly can't put it into words."

Then she gave Cole a sweet smile. "You should come inside for a minute."

The dog seemed to understand the invitation. It padded gamely into the living room.

Amber's cute, disheveled appearance, the mutt's claws clicking on the hardwood and the baby powder scent of Zachary's warm body curled in his arms brought a sense of unreality to Cole.

"Sure," he answered, and followed her through the archway.

It took only seconds for him to realize this was a perfect opportunity to learn more about her.

"It was either this or the mansion." She seemed to be apologizing for the opulent surroundings. "We thought it would be less disruptive if Zachary kept his nanny, Isabel. She occasionally sleeps over, so there was no way we'd all fit in my apartment. It's one bedroom with a tiny kitchen. This place belonged to Samuel."

The furnishings were obviously expensive, but they were strewn with baby blankets and rattles, the floor decorated with colorful plastic toys.

"Sorry about the mess," she said.

"You don't need to apologize."

"And me." She looked ruefully down at herself. "Well, this is me. This is what I normally look like. Last night was the anomaly."

"Seriously, Amber. You have nothing to apologize for. You look great."

She coughed out a laugh of disbelief.

"Okay, you look normal. How formal do you think we get in Alaska?"

She seemed to consider that. "Can I get you something?"

"I'm fine."

He didn't want to put her to any work. Then again, judging by Zachary's even breathing and relaxed body, his excuse for hanging around had just fallen asleep. Maybe refreshments weren't such a bad idea.

"Do you happen to have coffee?" he asked.

"Coming up. Take a seat anywhere." She gestured to the furniture as she exited through another archway that obviously led to the kitchen.

Cole took in the massive living room. In one corner, a plush sofa and a couple of leather armchairs bracketed a gas fireplace. Another furniture grouping was set up next to a bank of picture windows overlooking the city. The room was open to a formal dining room at one end and a hallway at the other that obviously led to the bedrooms.

He decided to follow Amber into the kitchen. No point in wasting valuable conversation time here by himself.

The kitchen was also huge, with high ceilings, a central island, generous granite counter spaces, stainless-steel appliances of every conceivable description and maple cabinets interspersed with big windows that faced the park. There was a breakfast nook at one end, stationed beside a balcony door, and an open door at the other, leading to a big pantry.

"This is very nice," said Cole.

"I'm still getting used to the size." She closed the lid and pressed a button on the coffeemaker. "It's weird moving into someone else's stuff—their furniture, their dishes, their towels. It's crazy, but I miss my pepper mill." She pointed to a corner of the counter. "You practically need a forklift to use that one."

Cole found himself smiling. "You should move your own stuff in."

For some reason, her expression faltered.

"I'm sorry," he quickly put in. "It's too soon?"

She paused, seeming to search for words. "It's too something. I won't pretend I was close to my stepsister, and I barely knew Samuel. Maybe it's the court case. Maybe I don't want to jinx anything. But I'm definitely keeping my own apartment intact until everything is completely finalized."

Cole perched on a stool in front of the island. Zachary was

quiet and comfortable in his arms and surprisingly easy to hold. "Tell me about the court case."

"You haven't read the tabloids?"

"Not much."

"I'm in a custody battle with Roth Calvin. He's a vice president at Coast Eagle and Samuel's stated choice for guardian."

"I'd heard that much."

"Coco named me as guardian, and I won on a technicality, but Roth's fighting it."

"Is Roth close to Zachary?"

Amber pulled two hunter-green stoneware mugs out of a side cupboard. "Roth's close to Coast Eagle. You were right last night in the car. The person who controls Zachary ultimately controls the company."

"So you *can* get me my Pacific routes." Now that Cole had thought it through, he realized the cover story was perfect. It gave him an excuse to ask all kinds of questions without anybody growing suspicious.

"I have no intention of micromanaging Coast Eagle."

"We had a fight last night, didn't we?" Cole had become so focused on the shoes, and then the dog, and then on Zachary, he'd forgotten she'd left the car mad at him.

"You call that a fight?"

"I believe I questioned your commitment to Zachary's inheritance."

"My commitment is to Zachary. I want the company to stay healthy for him, sure. But I can tell when I'm not the smartest person in the room. There are a lot of committed, hardworking managers and employees at Coast Eagle. They need to continue running the company."

"Don't sell yourself short."

"I'm an assistant director, Cole."

He liked it when she said his name. "You're responsible for the well-being of the company owner."

Her gaze rested on Zachary, and her tone went soft. "Poor thing."

"Poor little rich boy?" It came out more sarcastic than Cole had intended.

"I honestly wish he'd inherited a whole lot less. That way nobody would fight me for him."

"So you're afraid you might lose?"

Her expression faltered, and she focused on pouring the freshly brewed coffee. "I try not to think about it." She turned back with both cups in her hands. "I can't believe you got him to sleep."

"I'm just sitting here breathing. You wore him out."

"Maybe he likes the sound of your voice."

"Maybe," Cole agreed.

Cole didn't like to think Zachary's behavior had anything to do with the genetic connection. But Cole supposed it was possible he sounded like Samuel. Maybe Zachary was subconsciously picking it up.

"You can probably get away with putting him down in his bed," said Amber.

"He's fine here."

Oddly, Cole didn't want to put Zachary down, at least not right away. This vulnerable little baby was his brother. And for some reason, the kid had instantly trusted him. Cole was suddenly acutely aware that there were two of them in the world. He could not have imagined how that would make him feel.

Amber's boss, Herbert Nywall's, expression was stern as he rose from the table in her compact office on the seventh floor of the Coast Eagle building.

Max Cutter was the company's chief lawyer, so Herbert had had no choice but to acquiesce to his request to speak privately with Amber. But it was obvious Herbert was becoming frustrated with the increasing interruptions of Amber's day-to-day duties.

She didn't blame him.

"Can this wait, Max?" she asked, earning a look of shock from Herbert.

"I'm afraid not. Sorry, Herbert."

"Not at all," Herbert responded with false cheer. "She's all yours."

"We're pretty busy today," Amber told Max as Herbert closed the door behind him.

"You can't pretend this isn't happening." Max took the chair across from her at the two-person meeting table. It was wedged between her desk and a bookshelf in the windowless room.

"Believe me, I'm not pretending anything isn't happening." In the past three weeks, her life had been turned completely upside down.

Nothing was remotely normal, and now Cole Parker had appeared, somehow insinuating himself into the circumstances. She didn't quite know what to make of him. He was opportunistic, that was for sure. And he had definite designs on Coast Eagle.

But Zachary's reaction to him had been astonishing. And her own reaction was just as bizarre. Yesterday, she'd fought a ridiculous urge to throw herself into Cole's arms and trust him completely.

Max got straight to the point. "Roth's pressuring the board to appoint him president."

The news surprised Amber. It also worried her. "I thought they were going to wait to choose a president."

"That was the agreement. But he wants it bad, and half of the board members are convinced he'll win the custody battle. If he does, he'll be the guy deciding who stays on the board. They want to ingratiate themselves now while they have a chance."

Amber understood their dilemma. She even sympathized. If Roth obtained custody of Zachary, he'd be ruthless in his revenge on board members who'd stood against him.

"Plus," Max continued, "they see strength in him, decisiveness and intelligence. They think he'll make a good president."

"I don't like him," Amber blurted out. "And I don't think he'd make a good president."

Max sat back in his chair. "That was definitive." He seemed to be considering her words. "Is it because of the situation with Zachary? Because that would certainly be understandable."

"It's because he recklessly spends company money. He wants to refurbish or replace the entire fleet with no regard whatsoever for the debt load. He's a shopaholic on a massive scale."

Max quirked a smile. "Interestingly put, but not inaccurate from what I've seen."

"They can't make him president."

"The board's deadlocked. We need to appoint another board member to break the tie."

Amber shook her head. Max had broached the subject of board appointments with her two weeks ago.

"You know I don't want to do that."

"I know you don't."

"I don't want to run Coast Eagle." She knew she wasn't qualified to take the helm of the company.

"Well, you're the only one who doesn't."

Amber came to her feet, taking the three steps that brought her flush against the front of her desk. She turned back. This was a terrible office for pacing.

Max spoke again. "If you appoint the right person, a majority will agree on a different interim president and Roth will have to back down. If you don't appoint anyone, MacSweeny will flip. It's only a matter of time. And then Roth's in."

Amber spoke more to herself than to Max. "And the spending spree begins."

For some reason, her thoughts turned back to Cole Parker. In the car Saturday night, he'd said it was her responsibility to take control of the company for Zachary. She'd disagreed with him at the time, but the advice stuck with her.

She let the memory take shape, and his image came clear in her mind. The streetlights had played across his handsome face. He was sexy in a suit, sexier still in his blue jeans the next morning at the penthouse. And the memory of him holding Zachary? The tenderness had touched a chord deep down inside her. It shouldn't have turned her on, but it did. The truth was, everything about Cole turned her on.

All that probably meant she *shouldn't* take his advice.

She looked at Max, bringing herself back to the present. She had to agree that letting Roth plunge the airline into debt wasn't in Zachary's best interest. Any thinking person could see that. And what Max said was true. At the moment, she was the only person who could legally appoint a new board member.

If she didn't do it, no one could.

"Who?" she found herself venturing. "If I was to appoint someone, who would that be?"

It had to be someone they could trust. It also had to be someone who didn't have to fear Roth if he won the custody battle. It had to be someone who understood the airline, who brought true value to the board and who could be strong in the face of divided loyalties, uncertain times and extraordinarily high stakes.

She couldn't think of a single person who fit the bill.

"You," Max told her softly.

"No." She gripped the back of her chair and shook her head. "No." It was unthinkable. *"No."*

"You underestimate yourself, Amber."

"Coco chose me because she knew I would love Zachary. She had no idea it would put me in this position with the company."

"Coco had no idea about anything," said Max.

Amber didn't know how to respond to that. Her sister wasn't the most analytical person in the world. It was fair to say that Coco had operated on emotion rather than logic. It was also fair to say that Coco had never really grown up. She'd wanted what she'd wanted, and she'd usually wanted it right away. She'd never spent much time worrying about the impact on others.

"There's no one else," said Max, spreading his palms.

"There has to be."

"It's one vote. You take the appointment. You go to one meeting. You vote. You leave. And the new president takes over the reins." He glanced around her small office, all but wrinkling his nose. "You can come back here an hour later and take over your regular duties."

"There's nothing wrong with my job."

"Nobody's saying there is. Though not many new billionaires would keep working in this particular office."

"I'm not a new—"

"Amber, please. I can see that your instinct is to be humble. But you're Zachary's guardian. Anytime you want to exercise it, you have control of a billion-dollar company."

"Temporarily."

"Maybe. But maybe not."

She slid back into her chair, propping her elbows on the table. "It's not that simple."

"It's very simple."

She couldn't, wouldn't, didn't dare let her head run away with any aspect of the situation. There was too much at stake for her to let her guard down.

She tried to explain her feelings to Max. "I can't let myself think it's real until it's really real. You know?"

"Amber, this is no time to be superstitious."

"I can't jinx custody of Zachary. I can lose anything else, but not him."

"Coast Eagle needs you to step up."

Her stomach went hollow, and her pulse began to pound. It wasn't exactly what Cole had said, but it was close. Two apparently smart men were telling her the same thing.

"How long do I have to decide?"

"Twenty-four hours. After that, we may lose MacSweeny."

"Let me think about it."

Max gave a sharp nod. Then he rose. "I'll be back tomorrow."

"I'll be here."

"Max is a very intelligent lawyer," said Destiny over Zachary's cries.

They were in the penthouse kitchen, Amber jostling Zachary and Destiny doling out linguini and salad.

"You're a smart lawyer, too," said Amber.

"Sure, but I'm looking after your interests. Max is looking after the interests of Coast Eagle. From the perspective of what's in the best interests of the company, you should absolutely take the board appointment."

"And from the perspective of me?"

"You'll make a lifelong enemy out of Roth."

"I've done that simply by breathing."

Destiny grinned, while Zachary's cries increased.

Amber jiggled harder. She was growing exhausted. "I swear, if I had Cole Parker's phone number, I'd call him up and beg him to come over."

"He's the other Alaska guy?"

"Yes, the one who put Zachary to sleep Sunday morning without lifting a finger." Amber knew she should feel miffed by that, because it sure didn't seem fair.

Destiny picked up her phone. "I've got Luca's number."

"Yeah, right," Amber chuckled.

But Destiny raised her phone to her ear. "Luca? It's Destiny."

"Don't you dare," said Amber.

Destiny stopped talking and smiled. "Thanks."

Amber shook her head in warning.

"That's not why I'm calling," said Destiny. "No. It's really not. I'm looking for Cole."

Amber shook her head more frantically, moving closer.

"Not even close," said Destiny. "Tell him Amber needs him to put Zachary to sleep."

"She's joking," Amber called out, causing Zachary to cry louder. She turned away, walking toward the living room. "Shh, shh, shh," she whispered in his ear. "I'm sorry, baby. I didn't mean to scare you."

"Hi, Cole," said Destiny from behind her. "Yes, Amber needs the baby cavalry. Can you come?"

Amber couldn't believe this was happening. Cole was a stranger. You couldn't ask a stranger to drop everything, drive over and soothe your baby. The world didn't work like that. With any luck at all, he'd be bright enough to say no.

"They're on their way," called Destiny.

"You've lost your mind."

Destiny set down her phone and moved to the wine rack recessed in the kitchen wall. "How's Zachary been doing with the nanny?"

"Sometimes he's good with Isabel, sometimes not. Evening

is always the worst. We're been helping each other, but tonight's her night off."

Perusing the shelves, Destiny chose a bottle. "Do you think maybe we could give him a little of the merlot?"

"I wish. But definitely pour me a glass."

Destiny located the corkscrew, peeled the foil and opened the bottle. She moved two glasses to the center of the island and poured, placing them next to the two plates of linguini.

Then she slid onto a stool while Amber jiggled her way back to the island.

Amber knew there was no point in sitting down. Zachary had a built in altimeter. His preferred height was precisely five feet off the ground, not four feet, not four and a half. And his preferred swaying arc was approximately nine inches. Any deviation from the pattern brought an immediate vocal protest.

Luckily, Amber had become adept at simultaneously standing, swaying and eating. She lifted her fork and swirled a bite of the seafood linguini.

"Say I was to appoint myself to the board," she ventured.

"Say you were."

"Would it hurt my custody argument? I mean, would it look like I was the kind of person who used Zachary to gain power in Coast Eagle?"

Destiny thought for a moment. "Maybe. I mean, we'd spin it that you were willing to step up and look after Zachary's interests."

"Would a judge believe that?"

"Maybe. It's a fifty-fifty shot. Then again, a judge might just as easily take you *not* joining the board as a sign you weren't a suitable guardian."

"Problem is we can't separate the two." Amber set down her fork to free her hand for a drink of wine.

Zachary batted his arm out, nearly knocking the glass from her hand. She gave up on the drink.

"If you do it," said Destiny, "Roth will spin it that you're power hungry. If you don't, he'll spin it that you're incapable. But Coco wanted you, and that's important."

"But Samuel wanted Roth."

"He did," Destiny agreed.

"And in a character and intellect debate, Samuel is going to win out over Coco every time."

Destiny took a drink, and Amber couldn't help but feel envious. She settled for another bite of the linguini.

A knock sounded on the door.

"That was fast," said Amber, starting for the path through living room.

"They're staying at the East Park."

With a tired and tearful Zachary on her shoulder, Amber crossed to the entry hall. She checked the peephole and opened the door to Cole and Luca.

She couldn't help but smile at the sight of the dog at Cole's heels. He'd told her about the shoe altercation, and his decision to take the animal back to the hotel. She also knew he'd been planning to drop the scruffy dog at a shelter. He hadn't done it yet, and that was somehow endearing.

His expression was sympathetic as he gazed at the pathetically sobbing Zachary.

"I hear you've got trouble?" he said.

Zachary instantly perked up. He straightened in Amber's arms, turning to Cole and blinking his watery eyes. Then he lunged for him.

Cole reflexively reached out, stepping forward to catch the baby. "Hey there, partner."

"It's hard not to take this personally," said Amber, even though her arms and shoulders were all but singing in relief as the weight was removed.

For some reason, Luca was grinning ear to ear as he took in the sight of Cole and Zachary. "Nice to see you again, Amber."

"Hello, Luca. I'm really sorry that Destiny called you guys. It wasn't a fair thing to do."

"No problem at all," said Luca. "She in here?" He brushed past Amber.

The dog kept his position next to Cole.

"In the kitchen," Amber called to Luca's back.

Cole moved into the entry, and Amber shut the door behind him. Zachary heaved a shuddering sigh and laid his head on Cole's shoulder.

"Do babies always react to you like this?" she couldn't help asking.

"I don't know. I'm not usually around them. Mostly, they ignore me."

"Do you mind if I have something to eat while you hold him?"

"Not at all." Cole shrugged out of his jacket, draping it over the brass coat tree. "Do whatever you want. Have a bath. Take a nap."

"Tempting," Amber admitted. "But I've got a glass of merlot in there with my name on it."

Cole and the dog followed her into the kitchen, where Destiny had dished up some linguini for Luca.

"Peace and quiet," she noted, taking in Zachary's posture. His little hand was stroking one side of Cole's neck, his face buried in the other.

"Hungry?" Amber asked Cole.

"You go ahead. But I'd pour myself a glass of wine." He took the remaining of the four stools, and the dog curled up at his feet.

Amber took a satisfying sip of wine and another bite of linguini. It was wonderful to have the use of both hands.

"What's his name?" Destiny nodded to the dog as she poured wine for the men.

"I don't know," said Cole, looking down. "We met in the alley after the dance, and I wasn't really planning to keep him."

"I think he's planning to keep you," said Amber.

"That's because I fed him a burger that first night."

"Cole's got plenty of room in Alaska," said Luca.

"You're taking him home with you?" asked Destiny.

Cole glanced down and seemed to contemplate. "I suppose I am. I'm not liking his chances stacked up against those adorable puppies at the shelter. I don't know who would choose him."

"He's not that homely." Amber sized up the square, tan muzzle, the floppy, uneven ears and wiry, mottled coat. "Okay, maybe Alaska's not such a bad idea."

"You're so diplomatic," Cole said with a smile.

"He'll need a name," said Amber.

"Rover?" Cole asked the dog.

It didn't react.

"Spot?"

Nothing.

Amber smiled as she ate and drank.

"Lucky? Butch? Otis?"

The dog glanced sharply up.

"Seriously?" asked Cole. "Otis?"

The dog came up on its haunches and lifted its chin.

"Otis wins," said Destiny.

"Otis it is," said Cole, reaching down to pat the dog's head.

It sniffed at Zachary's bare foot.

Zachary looked down with curiosity, and the two stared at each other for a long moment.

"Sizing up the competition?" said Destiny.

"Which one?" asked Amber.

Zachary looked suspicious of Otis, and Otis looked suspicious of Zachary. The adults all chuckled at the picture.

Amber quickly polished off her dinner, knowing it wasn't fair to take continued advantage of Cole.

She moved her plate to the sink. "I should give this little guy his bath."

"I'm guessing you mean Zachary and not Otis," said Luca.

"Definitely Zachary." She couldn't help but picture Coco's reaction to Otis in her expensive bathtub.

Cole shifted Zachary on his lap. "Otis had a bath in the hotel car wash the first night I found him."

"Did he mind?" asked Amber.

"Didn't seem to. He smelled pretty bad, so I bribed the valet."

She couldn't help admire his ingenuity.

"Smells a little like Showoff Gold now, but it's a big improvement."

Zachary reached for Otis, grabbing a handful of his ear.

"Careful there," said Cole, gently pulling Zachary back. But Otis just gazed at Zachary, not seeming the slightest bit concerned.

Much as Amber hated to disturb Zachary when he seemed so happy, it was getting late. She moved toward him.

"Time for a bath?" she asked, a lilt to her voice as she smiled brightly, trying to send him the message that something fun was about to happen.

She held out her arms. "Bath?"

Zachary shrank against Cole, his face scrunching up in discontent.

"I can come with you," Cole offered.

"That seems like a cop-out," said Amber. She was already feeling a bit inadequate as a guardian.

Cole rose. "It's a bath. No big deal. Sometimes it's good to just go with the flow."

She couldn't deny she was tempted. "Okay, maybe just this once. But I'm supposed to be convincing a judge that I'm the best guardian for Zachary. I'd hate to have to tell him it was you instead."

"Definitely just this once," Cole answered. "I can hardly give the kid a bath from Alaska."

"In that case, let's make my evening easier."

She led the way down the hall to the main bathroom.

It was easy to tell which of the rooms had been redecorated by Coco. The living room and kitchen were luxurious, with the finest appliances and handcrafted furnishings. But they were subdued and sophisticated, with the obvious touch of a professional decorator.

The master bedroom and the three bathrooms were in stark contrast. They were bright and flamboyant, every feature an extravagance of brilliance and color.

"I should probably prepare you for this," she told Cole.

He was behind her in the wide hallway, followed by Otis.

"I don't mind a mess," he answered.

Amber couldn't help but laugh. "I wish I was talking about a mess."

The bathrooms were very well cared for. Samuel had employed the same housekeeper at the penthouse for nearly a decade, and Amber had no intention of letting the efficient woman go. She paused with her door on the handle.

"What's wrong?" Cole asked.

"It's purple."

"Okay?"

"Very purple." She pushed the door wide and pressed the light switch, watching for his reaction.

The floor tiles were a deep, mottled violet. The wallpaper was mauve with violet pinstripes. Two ultramodern sinks were purple porcelain on clear glass.

The skylight glowed with perimeter lighting, while spotlights twinkled above the shower, sinks and tub. In addition to the complex purple tile work, the walls were decorated with pink-hued abstract paintings, while violet-scented candles and whimsical figurines were placed on glass tables.

"This is very purple," Cole agreed, moving inside as he gazed around in obvious amazement.

She followed. "The tub in here is a relatively manageable size."

She pushed up the sleeves of her sweater and twisted the taps on the oval tub. "The one in the master bedroom is nearly a pool."

Cole grinned. "I guess if you've got the money, you can do whatever turns your crank."

Straightening, Amber retrieved a couple of thick towels and a facecloth from a recessed cabinet, balancing them next to a pink porcelain cat. For all its size, the room was hopelessly impractical. There was only one small cabinet, and the counter space was minimal, most of it taken up with decorations.

"It was pretty interesting to see what Coco did when she was suddenly presented with money," said Amber.

"Did you offer your opinion?" Cole asked, shaking his head at the outlandish decor.

"I didn't see this room until after she died."

Cole perched himself on the edge of the tub and began to

pop the snaps on Zachary's one-piece suit. "But you don't think your stepsister handled money very well?"

"I think it overwhelmed her. She grew up in downtown Birmingham without a lot of advantages. She was nineteen when she met Samuel."

"He must have been fifty."

"At least."

There was an edge to Cole's voice. "Nice."

"She was pretty, stunningly beautiful, actually. She was outgoing and fun loving, and she seemed to idolize Samuel. I'm sure a psychologist would have a field day with the relationship."

"I'm sure," Cole agreed.

Amber knelt down and tested the water temperature with the inside of her wrist. She shut off the taps. Then she suction cupped Zachary's bath safety ring to the bottom of the tub and dropped a couple of brightly colored plastic fish into the water.

"Based on my single college psychology elective," said Amber as Cole lowered the naked Zachary into the ring, "I would say Samuel was everything Coco's father was not. Conversely, I suspect Samuel secretly feared he'd never have children and saw Coco as someone he could care for and protect."

"And sleep with," said Cole.

"He did marry her. I have to give him credit for that."

Zachary grabbed for the green fish, sending splashes of water over the edge of the tub, dampening Amber's sweater and jeans.

"To be fair," she continued, "from what I saw, he genuinely loved Zachary. I think he'd have had more children if Coco was willing."

Cole had gone silent, his attention fixed on the baby.

After a long moment, he spoke. "You liked Samuel?"

"Not really. I mean, I barely knew him, but it's hard to admire a fiftysomething man who marries a nineteen-year-old. Especially one who…" Amber tried to reframe her thought, but there was no way to put it that wasn't insulting to Coco.

She stretched to retrieve the facecloth, dampening it in the bathwater then squirting some rose-scented soap from a china dispenser.

"So how is it that you and Coco became stepsisters?" Cole asked.

Amber started to wash Zachary's back, relieved that he'd let her blow past the nonanswer. "My mother died when I was a baby. When I was seven, my father remarried. But shortly after, he was killed by a drunk driver, and then it was just Tara and me."

"I'm sorry to hear that."

"Thank you." At first, Amber had been inconsolable over the loss of her father, while Tara had seemed overwhelmed by the responsibility of Amber. So Amber had grown up fast, accepted the situation and learned to be strong.

She continued with the story. "Shortly after he died, Tara remarried and got pregnant with Coco."

"Did you and Tara have a good relationship?"

Zachary splashed happily, cooing in the tub while Amber washed him.

"We didn't fight or anything. She worked as a waitress. I was in after-school care. She made sure I was fed and had clothes. Meanwhile I was a pretty good kid, and stayed out of her way."

"That sounds lonely."

Amber shrugged. "It was okay. I didn't really know any different until Coco came along." She dampened Zachary's soft hair and rubbed in a dollop of baby shampoo.

"What happened?"

"I saw a different approach to parenting."

"Let me guess, Coco was the golden child."

"She was the princess of the family. She was their biological baby. While I was ten and didn't belong to either of them."

"I'm so sorry, Amber."

She gave herself a mental shake as she removed Zachary from the bath ring. "It was a very long time ago. I don't know why I'm even going into it."

"Because I asked."

Crouched over the tub, she leaned Zachary along her arm to rinse his hair. He squirmed but didn't cry.

"I never knew my father," Cole said from beside her.

"Divorce?" she asked.

"Yes. Before I was born."

"Did you have a relationship with him?"

"None."

"Why not?"

"My mother wanted nothing to do with him, and neither did I."

"Do you still feel the same way?"

"I do. But it wouldn't matter."

Amber guessed at what Cole meant. "He passed away?"

"He did."

She stood Zachary up, checking to make sure he was squeaky-clean. "Any regrets?

"Not a one. He never knew about me. My mom was absolutely fantastic. It was just the two of us, but she was hardworking, loving, supportive."

"That's nice to hear." Amber lifted Zachary from the tub, wrapping him in a fluffy mauve towel.

He cooed happily, but then spotted Cole. He wriggled in her lap, reaching out and whimpering.

"This is definitely insulting," she said.

"You're great with him."

"I'm not sure about that." She was honest. "But I'm what he's got, and I do love him."

Cole rose from the edge of the tub, reaching out to take Zachary in one arm and then helping her to her feet. It took him a minute to speak.

"Sometimes," he said softly, "families just happen."

His hand was warm and dry beneath hers, broad, strong and slightly callused. He didn't immediately let her go, and a strange feeling surged up her arm, pushing into her chest.

Time seemed to stop. She stood still and drank in his appearance. He was such a gorgeous, sexy man. His smoke-gray eyes were warm with emotion. She noticed once again that his shoulders were broad, arms strong, chest deep. He seemed to radiate a power that was more than just physical.

She fought another urge to throw herself into his arms.

"Amber," he breathed.

He lifted his hand to brush her damp hair from her cheek.

His touch was featherlight, but she felt herself sway toward him.

He leaned in, slowly, surely.

Then he touched his lips to hers.

He tasted like fine wine, his lips warm and firm. The scented steam rose between them while his fingers slipped back, delving into her hair.

The kiss deepened, and her desire skyrocketed.

"Gak," called Zachary, his hand smacking her ear.

She jerked back in shock.

"Gak," Zachary repeated, pressing his feet against her as if he needed space.

"All right, partner," said Cole. "You have my attention." But his gaze stayed fixed on Amber.

Embarrassment flooded her. "I don't know what happened there."

"I do," said Cole. He held her gaze for a long beat. "And I've never taken a single psychology course."

Then he backed away to the bathroom door, leaving her awash in arousal and confusion.

Four

Cole sat across from Luca at a small table in the festively decorated lobby lounge in the East Park Hotel. A blue-and-silver Christmas tree towered thirty feet above them. Lit reindeer bracketed the entrance. Strings of garland and clusters of icicles cascaded from the high ceilings, while the windows were frosted with scenes of ice and snow.

Carols played softly in the background as guests enjoyed the breakfast buffet.

"There's not a doubt in my mind that Amber is the right guardian for Zachary," said Cole.

He couldn't help but worry about Amber's description of her stepsister, and how Roth's legal team might use Coco's background and reputation. Amber was definitely going to have a fight on her hands in court.

"This is what I'm talking about," said Luca, seeming not to have heard Cole's comment as he swiveled his laptop around to face Cole. "That's Samuel at the age of thirty-three, a year older than you are now."

Cole focused on the picture of his biological father. The eyes were similar, but Samuel's hair was lighter, his chin narrower and his nose had a bit of an upturn.

"It's only there if you're looking for it," he said. "And nobody's looking for it."

"You've been outed by a nine-month-old baby."

"Yeah, well, I think we can count on him to keep quiet."

"He'll learn to talk someday."

"Not before I leave town."

"And listen to this." Luca turned the laptop and punched another key. "It's Samuel giving a speech twenty years ago."

"…once the plan is fully implemented, the new routes will take us to Britain, France and Germany…"

"Okay, that's a bit uncanny," Cole had to admit. He'd heard

his own voice recorded on numerous occasions, and Samuel's was very, very close.

"The kid knows you're family."

"At least that explains why he's latched on to me."

Luca took a sip of his coffee. "But you're still just going to walk away?"

"No."

Luca drew back in clear astonishment. "You're not?"

"First, I'm going to make sure Amber wins custody. Then I'm going to walk away. Involving myself in the Henderson family was never part of the plan."

Cole was heading back to his life in Alaska just as soon as things were under control here. Showing up in Atlanta was about him doing his duty. It wasn't some family reunion, and he wasn't about to upend his and Zachary's lives by acknowledging their biological connection.

Kissing Amber last night might have momentarily thrown him off track. He still couldn't believe he'd done it—in a purple bathroom of all places, with Zachary in his arms. How ridiculous was that?

His plan was to keep complications to a minimum. Not that a single kiss had added some huge complication. In fact, he'd already put it into perspective.

Sure, Amber was pretty. She was sweet and kind and compassionate. And she'd had a rough time of it growing up. Her stories had engaged his sympathies.

But lots of people had a less-than-stellar upbringing. She was fine now, and she loved Zachary. And Cole was right to leave the two of them to get on with it.

"You're sure that's what you want?" asked Luca.

"I'm positive it's what I want." Cole pulled his thoughts back to his earlier point. "Roth will try to prove that Coco was unfit to name either a guardian for Zachary or the person to control Coast Eagle."

"On the bright side," said Luca, "I don't think many wills are overturned because they're foolish."

"I hope not." Just then, Cole wished he knew more about the law.

"So what do you think of Destiny?" he asked Luca. "I mean, other than she's hot. Can you see past the fact that she's hot? Because you should declare a conflict of interest if you can't be objective." Cole wanted to be sure Amber was getting the best possible legal advice.

Luca was all but laughing as he cut into his waffle. "I don't need to declare a conflict of interest. I know she's smart."

"Are you sure? How do you know?"

"I asked her a few questions last night."

"And?"

"And she had a ton of technical information at her fingertips. But she wouldn't tell me anything about Amber specifically."

"You didn't make her suspicious, did you?"

"No. I pretended I was curious about what I'd read on social media. There's a lot out there on social media." Luca set down his cutlery and pressed a few more keys on the laptop. "For example, this, here. There are new rumors that Roth Calvin will be named interim president of Coast Eagle."

Cole reached out to turn the laptop to face him again. "I thought Amber was in charge?" Letting Roth step up as interim president couldn't be a good move for her.

"It's a board decision," said Luca.

"Which tells us Roth has the ear of the board." Cole didn't like the thought of that.

"It does seem like he's got the power at least temporarily."

Cole dropped his napkin onto the table and stood. "I need to get a handle on the guy."

"Where are you going?"

"Coast Eagle's corporate headquarters. I want to look Roth Calvin in the eyes."

"Right now? Without an appointment?"

"I'll talk my way in. I'm a fellow airline owner."

"You want some help?"

Cole considered the offer. But then he shook his head. "He's less likely to have his guard up if it's just one guy."

"Whatever you want."

Cole shrugged into his jacket. "See what else you can find out about the law."

"Can I talk to Destiny again?"

"As long as you're oblique."

Luca's eyes lit up. "Covert operations. Roger that. This is kind of fun."

Cole couldn't help but grin in return. "Seduce her if you have to."

"I'm all in for you, buddy."

Cole skirted the Christmas tree, made his way past the reindeer and exited to the sidewalk. It was easy to hail a cab, and it was a short ride to Coast Eagle.

He took a few fast steps across the lobby, purposefully blending in with a group of employees to pass unnoticed by the security counter. Then he entered the elevator, pretending he knew exactly what he was doing. Taking the chance that Roth's office would be on the top floor, he pressed the button.

The rest of the group exited on twelve. Cole continued up to a big, brightly lit reception area. It had gleaming hardwood floors, a bank of windows overlooking the city and a pair of immaculate saltwater fish tanks bracketing a long reception counter staffed by one woman.

"Good morning." She was immaculately dressed and thirty-something, and she smiled as she greeted him.

Cole strode forward and held out his hand. "Good morning. I'm Cole Parker, owner of Aviation 58. We're a midsize commercial airline out of Alaska. I was told Roth Calvin was the man to speak with at Coast Eagle."

"Do you have an appointment, sir?"

"I'm afraid I just got into town."

The woman's smile faded a little. "I'm sorry, but Mr. Calvin doesn't have any openings today."

Footfalls and male voices rose up behind them. The woman's surreptitious, worried glance to the group told Cole one of them was likely Roth Calvin.

He quickly turned, talking the man in the middle of the group to be the guy in charge. It had to be Roth.

Again, Cole strode forward, offering his hand. "Roth Calvin. I'm Cole Parker."

Roth's expression was guarded, and his critical glance flicked to the receptionist. Cole figured it was only a matter of moments before security arrived on the scene.

"I was speaking with Amber Welsley the other day. She suggested you were the person to discuss Coast Eagle's Pacific routes? I'm Cole Parker, Aviation 58 out of Alaska."

"Amber told you to see me?" Roth asked.

"She did," Cole lied. "She speaks very highly of you."

Roth's eyes narrowed, and Cole feared he might have gone too far. He was trying to arouse Roth's curiosity, and maybe put him off guard with the mention of Amber.

Roth looked at Cole. Then he looked to the receptionist. "Sandra, push the Millsberg meeting by fifteen minutes."

"Yes, sir," the receptionist answered.

"Right this way, Mr. Parker." Roth gestured to a doorway off the reception area.

"Please, call me Cole." Cole entered an airy meeting room that housed a round table for four with leather and chrome chairs, coffee service on a marble side counter and a sofa grouping near the picture windows.

Roth gestured to one of the chairs at the round table, then took the one opposite. "How can I help you, Cole?"

"I understand you're about to be named interim president," Cole opened.

A smug smile formed on Roth's face. "You've been listening to rumors."

"I find, more often than not, rumors tend to be based on some truth. I'll be honest, Roth, Aviation 58 is looking to expand along the West Coast. With the shakeup at Coast Eagle, I wondered if you might be interested in discussing some of your less-profitable routes in the West."

"All of our routes are profitable."

Cole had checked out Coast Eagle's public information on

the ride over, and now he made some assumptions and guesses. "Seattle to Vancouver is barely break-even. You've been losing market share in Portland. And your passenger load is low on anything northbound out of LA. Entering into a lease or code-share deal with Aviation 58 could boost your cash flow and profits considerably."

"You've done your homework, I see."

"I have," said Cole. "And it tells me Amber Welsley is a short-term play. You're the guy with the ear of the board."

Roth didn't answer, but he did nod.

"I haven't seen the actual will, of course. But I can guess where that's going. A trophy wife is all well and good, but nobody's under any illusions. Samuel would never have allowed a situation where Coco's decisions could run Coast Eagle into the ground."

Roth chuckled, and his expression relaxed. "You strike me as an intelligent man, Cole Parker."

"I'm also a patient man. I get that your attention has to be on the home front for a few months."

Roth gave a shrug. "These things can be expedited."

"That's good to hear."

"A word here, a conversation there. It's all about who you know, and who knows you."

"I understand," said Cole. "The sooner you get custody of the kid, the better." He paused. "I mean, the better for Coast Eagle, of course."

"Once the big question is settled, we will be looking for an early cash influx," said Roth, coming to his feet.

Cole rose with him. "That's good to hear, I'll—"

Suddenly, the meeting room door flung open, and Amber burst in. She glared at Cole, cheeks flushed, nostrils flared. "You went behind my back?"

"Amber." Roth's voice was stern and patronizing.

"You suggested I follow-up," Cole said to Amber, purposefully mischaracterizing their conversation.

"This is a private meeting, Amber." Roth's tone grated on Cole's nerves.

Amber ignored Roth and spoke to Cole. "I suggested you follow up with Joyce Roland."

"Amber," Roth all but shouted. "Can you please *excuse us?"*

Cole had to steel himself from demanding that Roth shut up.

The receptionist appeared in the doorway. "Mr. Calvin? They're waiting. The Millsberg meeting?"

Roth looked to Cole. "I do apologize."

"No problem. Thank you for seeing me. I'll be in touch."

Roth looked to Amber, obviously waiting for her to leave.

She folded her arms across her chest, standing her ground. Cole wanted to applaud.

Roth gave in and left the room, followed by the receptionist.

"How dare you," Amber whispered.

Cole wished he could tell her he was on her side. "It was an initial courtesy call. Nothing sinister. I told you up front that I was interested in the Pacific routes."

"And what were you doing last night? Pumping me for information? Are you actually using Zachary's trust to gain an inside advantage?"

"You called *me* last night," he reminded her.

"And you were only too happy to show up."

"To help with Zachary."

"That's how you played it, all right." There was something in her eyes, a veiled hurt that made him think of their kiss.

He took a step forward. "Amber, I'm sorry."

"For lying to me?"

"I didn't lie to you. Last night was all about Zachary." He paused. "I mean, it was *mostly* all about Zachary."

She gave her hair a little toss. "You don't need to explain."

But he did need to explain. He wanted to explain. "I like you, Amber."

"Well, I don't like you."

He moved closer anyway. "Yes, you do."

"Go away."

He shook his head. "I understand that it's complicated."

"It's not complicated."

"It's Zachary. It's business. It's you, and it's me." Even as he spoke the words, he asked himself what on earth he thought he was doing. He needed to leave this alone, not ramp it up.

"There is no you and me." But her expression instantly shifted, telling him otherwise. Her lips parted, her blue-eyed gaze going bedroom soft.

Cole glanced at the open door, debating pushing it closed and pulling her into his arms again. But that would be a stupid move. The receptionist, Sandra, would certainly report the closed door to Roth. It would complicate things even further for Amber.

But she was so enchanting, and his memory of kissing her was so incredibly strong, he couldn't stop himself. He reached past her and gave the door a shove. Her eyes went wide as it clicked shut.

Without giving her a chance to protest, Cole pulled her into his arms, bringing his thirsty lips down to hers and kissing her soundly. She gasped, but she didn't pull away. After a moment, her lips softened. She kissed him back, and her arms wound around his neck.

He pressed their bodies close together, feeling the sweet heat of her thighs and the softness of her breasts. He teased her lips with his tongue, and she responded, parrying with him, a small moan burbling in the back of her throat.

His hand went to her cheek, cradling the soft skin, holding her in place while he plundered her mouth. He forgot where they were, forgot everything except the sweet taste and scent of Amber. His other hand moved to her waist, sliding beneath her linen blazer, along her silk blouse, feeling the heat of her skin through the thin fabric.

Suddenly, she pushed back. "We can't."

Cole sucked in a breath. Of course they couldn't. What was he thinking? They were in her place of business.

"I'm sorry," he said.

But she shook her head. "My fault, too." Then she glanced at her watch. "I have to go. There's a board meeting." She stopped talking. Inhaled a deliberate breath and took a step back. "That was foolish. I don't know what got into me."

"Amber—"

"Goodbye, Cole." She moved for the door.

"Can I call you later?"

"No." She shook her head and pulled open the door.

From behind her desk, Sandra's sharp gaze went to Amber, then to Cole. He tried to look casual, innocent, as if nothing more than a brief conversation had taken place between them.

But it was hard to put his finger on the exact expression and posture that would convey those things. So he simply left the room, bid a brief goodbye to Sandra and took the elevator back to the lobby.

Smoothing back her hair and mentally pulling herself together, Amber reached for the door handle to Coast Eagle's main boardroom.

She couldn't believe she'd kissed Cole again. She couldn't believe she'd done it in the office. And she sure couldn't believe she'd enjoyed it.

She tugged open the door.

"There you are," said Max, rising from his seat at the head of the long boardroom table.

The other eight members of the board nodded politely, their gazes fixed on her. They were all men, fortysomething to sixtysomething, longtime members of the Atlanta business community and the aviation industry. She knew most of them by sight, but she'd shared little more than a passing greeting with any of them.

Max moved away from the head chair, gesturing for her to sit down in it. "Please, Ms. Welsley."

She hesitated over the bold gesture, but Max gave her an encouraging smile.

She told herself she could do this. For Zachary, she could do this. She lifted her chin, walked forward and took the power chair.

Max took the chair to her right.

She stared down the center of the table, fixing her vision on the photograph of a red-and-white biplane at the far end of the room. She had no idea what to say.

Luckily, Max opened for her. "Per article 17.9 of the Coast Eagle Articles of Incorporation," he said, "Ms. Welsley is exercising her right as majority shareholder—"

"She's not the majority shareholder," said Clint Mendes.

Max peered at Clint. "According to the State of Georgia, she represents the majority shareholder."

"But that's under appeal," said Clint.

"And until that appeal is settled, Ms. Welsley represents the interests of Zachary Henderson. Now, as I was saying—"

The boardroom door swung abruptly open, revealing Roth in the threshold, his eyes wide, face ruddy, and his jaw clenched tight.

"Mr. Calvin," said Max, a clear rebuke in his tone. "I'm afraid this is a private meeting."

"Is this *a coup?*" Roth demanded.

A hush came over the room as everyone waited to see what Amber would do.

She immediately realized she had to step up. She couldn't let Max defend her against Roth. She was going to be a board member, and she had to stand her ground.

If she lost the court case, Roth would have her fired within seconds. He would have done that anyway. She had nothing left to lose.

She came to her feet, turning and squaring her shoulders. "Please leave the meeting, Roth."

The silence boomed around her.

Roth's jaw worked, his face growing redder. "Are you out of your—"

"Please leave," she repeated. "This meeting is for board members only."

"You're not a board member," Roth all but shouted.

"I'm the majority shareholder, Roth. That's as much as you need to know. *Now leave.*"

Nelson MacSweeny coughed, but said nothing.

Roth glared at the man.

Then he fixed a biting, narrow-eyed stare on Amber.

But he seemed to understand that he'd lost the round. He stepped back, banging the door shut.

Knees shaky, Amber sat down. Everyone was still looking down the table at her. But something in their expressions had changed.

It might have been her imagination, but there seemed to be a level of respect in their eyes. She gazed levelly back. Her heart was pounding and her palms were sweating, but she wasn't about to let anyone know that Roth had rattled her.

"Ms. Welsley is exercising her right to appoint herself as a board member," said Max. "As current majority shareholder, she will sit as chair. As chair, she will break any tie over the appointment of an interim president."

"So not Roth," said Clint.

"Then who are we talking about?" Nelson asked.

"Are we taking nominations?"

"I've given it a lot of thought," said Amber. "I'd like to discuss Max Cutter as the interim president."

Max drew back in his seat. "I can't—"

"Turns out you can," said Amber. "I spoke to a lawyer this morning."

"You'll have to leave the room for the discussion," Nelson said to Max.

Max fixed his shrewd gaze on Amber. She didn't flinch. If she could sit as chair of the board, then he could sit as president. There was no one else she'd trust.

"Very well," said Max. He rose and gathered his briefcase.

As he passed, he paused behind her and leaned down. "I guess we'll go down together."

She turned her head to whisper. "Then I guess you'd better help me win."

"I was always going to help you win." He gave her a friendly pat on the shoulder as he walked away.

The door closed behind him and another board member spoke up. He was Milos Mandell, a former commercial pilot and internet entrepreneur.

"Can we speak freely?" asked Milos.

"I would think we'd better," said Amber.

"You seem like you understand what you just did."

She couldn't help flexing a small, resigned smile. "I believe I know what I just did."

"He's going to come after you," said Nelson, clearly referring to Roth.

"He's right to go after her," said Clint, glancing around at his fellow board members. "This *is* a coup."

Milos sat forward. "The coup would have been Roth taking over as president without the support of the major shareholder."

Clint stared hard at Amber. "You're jumping the gun, and it's going to cost you."

"While Roth will know you sided with him, so I guess you're safe." She let her words sink in for a moment.

Clint was smart enough to realize the opposite was also true. Amber now knew he was in opposition to her.

His jaw dropped a fraction of an inch. "I don't mean… That is, I'm not…"

"Any discussion on Max?" Amber asked the group.

She didn't have time to worry about Clint. She needed to get Max settled in as president, then she needed to focus on the court case, do justice to her day-to-day work and make sure Zachary stayed clean, fed and as happy as possible. The alliances, machinations and power plays at Coast Eagle were going to have to take a backseat.

On the staircase in front of Coast Eagle headquarters, Cole appeared and fell into step beside Amber. It was six o'clock. She was exhausted, and he was the last person she wanted to see.

Ironically, he was also the person she most wanted to see. The conflicting reactions were due to the kiss they'd shared in the meeting room.

"I read the press release," he opened, turning right along with her as she headed down the crowded sidewalk toward the transit station.

"I think that was a good move," he continued. "There's an

element of risk, but there's nothing about this situation that's not risky."

She stopped to turn on him, forcing the flow of people to part around them. The man had gone behind her back, kissed her senseless, and now he wanted to analyze her business decisions? "Is that really what you want to say to me?"

Her words seemed to catch him off guard and he hesitated. Horns honked and engines revved on the street as cars breezed past.

"Yes," he answered.

"Well." She coughed out a chopped laugh. "It's so *very* nice of you to approve of my decision."

"Are you still upset?"

"I'm also tired, and I'm busy, and I'm going to miss my train."

"Then you should get moving."

He was right. She turned abruptly to march toward the station.

He kept pace. "I have a hard time believing the Hendersons don't have cars and drivers."

"Are you going to pretend it didn't happen?"

"That you joined the board of directors?"

She rolled her eyes.

"That I kissed you?" he asked.

"That you betrayed me."

"I didn't betray you. I told you I was after the Pacific routes."

"Don't pretend you're stupid, Cole. And don't pretend I'm stupid, either."

"You're not stupid."

"I know."

"Except when it comes to transportation. Can I offer you a ride home?"

"You cannot."

"Why?"

Because he had her rattled. The memory of his kiss had taunted her all afternoon long, messing with her concentration. She wanted to know the kiss had rattled him, too.

"It'll get you home faster," Cole offered reasonably. "You'll be able to spend more time with Zachary."

"Go away." She fixed her sights on the train platform.

"Not what I was planning."

"What were you planning?" The question was automatic, and she instantly regretted asking it.

She didn't care about his plans. She wanted him out of her life. At least, a part of her wanted him out of her life. The other part wanted him to kiss her again. She nearly groaned in frustration.

"You're having a tough week," he said. "You need to have some fun."

She dodged her way around a group of pedestrians, then skirted a trash can and a stroller. "What? This doesn't look like fun?"

"Well, I'm having fun."

"What do you want, Cole?"

"To take you on a date."

His words shocked her to a halt.

He took her arm and drew her under a shop awning, next to a brick wall and out of the flow of pedestrians. "I can only guess at how hard you're working and how tired you must be. I want to help you take a break. Come out with me tonight. Let's walk through Atlantic Station, see the lights, drink hot chocolate. Or we can go skating. You said skating was your favorite."

"I don't like you, Cole."

"To be fair, you don't know me."

"I know enough."

"You only think you know enough." His gaze captured hers again, and the noise and commotion of the sidewalk seemed to fade.

"I'll sweeten the pot," he said. "We'll go to the penthouse. I'll work my magic and put Zachary to sleep. Can Isabel stay for the evening?"

"You're bribing me?"

"Absolutely."

"Why, Cole? The jig is up. I know you were using me to worm your way into Coast Eagle."

"Amber, I don't need you to worm my way into Coast Eagle. I walked through the front door and got a meeting with the soon-to-be president without an appointment."

"Roth's not going to be president."

"Good decision."

"You just switch your opinion on a dime, don't you?"

"I never thought he should be president."

She didn't know what to say to that. She didn't care what Cole thought. Still, for some reason she was glad to hear him agree with her.

"You need to get out for a while," Cole continued. "Take a break. Forget about everything."

She fought a smile at the absurdity. "What I want to forget is you."

His expression faltered, and she felt a stab of guilt.

"I'm sorry to hear that, Amber."

She was sorry she'd said it.

Wait, no, she wasn't. No good could come of her attraction to him. A date? The idea was absurd. He lived in Alaska, and her life was a mess.

The best they could hope for was a one-night stand. Which, when she thought about it...

Hoo, boy. She reached out to grip the brick wall.

"You okay?"

"I'm perfectly fine." She paused. "No, make that confused. Why do you want to go out with me? And why do you still want to help me with Zachary?"

It took him a moment to shrug. "Why not? I like you, Amber. I like Zachary."

"That's too simple an explanation." Amber raked her hand through her hair to tame it in the freshening wind.

"I'm not complicated."

"I am."

"It's ice-skating, Amber. What could be simpler than ice-skating?"

"You're trying to get your hands on our Pacific routes."

"Only if you want to sell them."

"I don't."

"Fair enough. Did you know you missed your train?"

It was pulling smoothly away on the tracks. He really was the most infuriatingly distracting man.

"My car is only a block away. What do you say?"

She wanted to say yes. She suddenly, desperately wanted to leave her troubles behind for a few hours and go ice-skating with Cole.

She gave in. "Okay."

He grinned, and she couldn't shake the feeling she'd been outmaneuvered.

Five

As they passed by the lit trees that lined the outdoor skating rink, Cole turned backward so that he was facing Amber. She wore a short white puffy jacket, blue jeans and bright yellow knit hat.

"Impressive," she told him with a smile.

He was grateful that she seemed relaxed. "Hockey."

Since it was barely below freezing, he'd gone with a windbreaker and a bare head. The fresh air felt good in his lungs.

"You're a hockey player?"

"Snow and ice sports are big in Alaska. I also snowboard and ski cross-country." He glanced over his shoulder to make sure the path was still clear as they rounded a corner.

"I swim," she said.

"Competitively?"

"At resorts, usually in the leisure pool, sometimes on the lazy river."

He brought up a mental image. "Impressive."

"Yeah, I float with the best of them."

"I was picturing you in a little yellow bikini. It was very impressive."

"That's just mean."

"Why?"

"Because I'll never live up to your imagination."

"Sure you will." His gaze took a reflexive tour of her trim figure. "Wait a minute. Do you intend to try?"

She laughed, and he loved the sound.

"Not this time of year," she singsonged.

"If I come back in June?"

"Maybe." She twirled neatly around.

"You're pretty good yourself."

"Flatterer." But her smile was bright.

"You're beautiful, too."

"I'm not interested in a one-night stand."

The statement took him by surprise. "Excuse me?"

"Just so you know. I wouldn't want you to get to the end of the night and be disappointed."

"Is that what you think this is about?"

He didn't know whether to be insulted or just plain disappointed. He hadn't invited her out to get her into bed. But he didn't deny he'd give pretty much anything for an unbridled night of passion in her arms.

"You're not staying in Atlanta," she said.

"True," he agreed, even though he kind of now wished he was.

"And you're putting in an awful lot of effort flirting with me."

"Also true." But only because flirting with her was so much fun.

"So the options are limited."

"Maybe I'm trying to romance the Pacific routes out from under you."

"You know that will never work."

It was true. Cole couldn't imagine her falling for something so simplistic. Then again, he wasn't remotely interested in the Pacific routes.

He and Luca were following a carefully planned and meticulously orchestrated expansion scheme for Aviation 58. It was on track, and he had no intention of deviating from it for the next few years. He'd never make a knee-jerk decision based on random availability.

"You're great with Zachary, you know." Cole didn't want to talk business.

"*You're* great with Zachary. I'm mostly treading water." Then she frowned. "But if you're ever called to testify, the correct answer is that Amber is *fantastic* with Zachary."

"I've never seen such incredible natural mothering instincts," he said.

Her frown deepened. "I'm not his mother."

"I didn't mean that," Cole quickly corrected the innocent comment. "I only meant that it's obvious that you love him."

She skated in pensive silence for a moment, the lighthearted music and bright lights suddenly seeming out of place.

"I'm sorry," he offered, moving back to her side, reminding himself that she had grown up without the love of either of her natural parents.

"He's so young," she said softly. "He won't remember either of them."

Cole reached out and took her hand. "He'll remember you."

"It's not the same thing."

There was a deep sadness in her eyes, and it wasn't at all what he'd planned for her tonight.

"Hot chocolate?" he asked, nodding toward the strip of shops and cafés. "I'll spring for whipped cream and orange brandy."

Her expression relaxed again. "Sure."

They coasted to a stop, exchanged their skates for boots and made their way through the colored lights and happy crowds. It felt natural to take Amber's hand again as they strolled along the pedestrian street. He helped her pick out a stuffed dog and a soft rattle for Zachary. They waited while the clerk gift wrapped the toys, and Cole slung the package over his shoulder.

"That looks nice." He pointed across the street to a fenced restaurant patio with padded chairs and glowing propane heaters.

"Sold," said Amber.

They crossed through the crowds and were shown to a table near a festively lit garden.

He glanced at his watch. "I read there were fireworks at ten."

"Perfect timing." She glanced around. "I love it down here at Christmas."

"There's nothing like this in Juneau."

"Too cold?"

"During the holidays, yes. We do fireworks on the Fourth of July, but they lose something since it doesn't get completely dark at night."

"Not at all?"

"A sort of twilight look around 2:00 a.m. But you can golf at midnight on the solstice."

"I can't even picture it. Do you like living there?"

"I love living there. Juneau has a great sense of community."

"Tell me about your mother."

Cole brought up fond memories. "She was very pretty. She was kind and cheerful. She worked hard. Looking back, I realize just how hard she had to work when I was young."

"She never went after your father for support?"

"She didn't want him to know I existed."

The statement clearly piqued Amber's interest. "Why not?"

Cole immediately realized his mistake in letting Samuel get into the conversation. He purposely kept the rest of his answer casual. "She thought he'd be more trouble than he was worth."

Amber nodded her understanding. "I hear you."

How she said it made him wonder if she'd had bad experiences with men. He wanted to ask, but just then, the waitress arrived with magnificent mugs of hot chocolate, decorated with whipped cream and chocolate sprinkles.

"Dessert in a cup," said Amber with a happy smile.

Cole took the opportunity to shift the conversation away from his father. "Tell me about your dad."

She thought for a moment while she spooned a dollop of the whipped cream into her mouth. "He was tall. He had this booming, infectious laugh. I remember him flipping pancakes in the air, and how he used to trot around the yard, whinnying like a horse, with me on piggyback."

"Little girls like that?"

"I did."

"My mom baked bread on Friday nights," said Cole. "I'd hear her in the kitchen after I went to bed. She'd let it rise all night, then bake it in the morning. Best breakfast of the whole week."

"I'm trying to picture you young."

An image of Zachary came to his mind, and he hoped she wasn't trying to picture back that far. He'd hunted the internet for more photos of Samuel, found many and he realized there was a significant family resemblance. Then he'd had a friend back in Alaska send him some of his own baby pictures to compare to Zachary. They were all but identical.

Amber took another spoonful of the whipped cream. "I can't picture it. You must have always been old."

"Old? Thanks a lot."

"How old are you?"

"Thirty-two. You?" He already knew, but it seemed logical to ask.

"Thirty-one. So I guess you're not so old."

"Gee, thanks."

She grinned. "But I'm surprised you're not married, or at least in a relationship."

"There's no current or likely future Mrs.—" He caught himself. "Mrs. Parker. You?"

"Married?" she scoffed.

"I meant in a serious relationship?"

"Nope."

"What about in the past?"

"These questions are getting quite personal."

"They are, aren't they?" He didn't apologize or retract it.

She wrapped her hands around the mug. "Nobody of note." After a pause, she kept talking. "I left home right after high school, worked days, went to school at night to get my accounting designation. I might not be a vice president, but my job at Coast Eagle is significant."

He stirred the whipped cream into his hot chocolate. "I never doubted it was."

"I oversee six branch offices and several dozen staff members."

"Have I said something wrong?" He couldn't figure out what had made her defensive. He had nothing but admiration and respect for what she'd accomplished in her professional life.

She took a sip. "Not you. Roth, I guess. And some of the other executives. Sometimes I think they assume I'm just like Coco. They all knew her, while most of them had barely met me before the crash. They seem to have forgotten that I was at Coast Eagle before she met Samuel. I sometimes get the impression they think Coco got me the job."

He could imagine that would be frustrating.

"I decided the best defense was to ignore it," she continued. "And to do a good job, hard work and success would prevail and all that."

"Did it work?"

"Not really. And then the plane crashed. And now everyone thinks there's a ditz at the helm."

"They're wrong."

"They don't know that."

"Fair enough. But you know what I think?"

Her expression seemed to relax a little. "What do you think, Cole Parker?"

"I think they'd better learn. They'd better learn to respect your intelligence and your tenacity."

Anyone could see she was the perfect guardian for Zachary. The judge was going to see that, too. And soon she was going to be in charge of all of their lives.

"You're good for my ego, Cole."

"I'm trying."

"But, wow, did I ever get off topic." She took another sip. "That was a very roundabout way of explaining that I didn't have time for boyfriends. It's not that I never had offers."

"Of course you had offers." He couldn't figure out what made her so insecure. "You're amazing. And you're gorgeous. And I never meant for a second to hint that men didn't seek you out. I meant… Okay, I was fishing around for the competition."

She drew back. "Competition for *what?*"

"That didn't come out right. I'm attracted to you, Amber. I know I'm not staying in Atlanta. But I think of this as a date. And I guess it's a reflex for guys to wonder about who else might be out there in the wings."

"There are no wings. I mean, I have no wings. At least none with guys waiting in them." She closed her eyes and shook her head. "I'm making this worse and worse, aren't I?"

Cole struggled not to smile. "You're making it better and better."

"Tell me some more about you instead."

"Sure. What do you want to know?"

She settled back into the chair. "Women."

The first volley of fireworks burst in the night sky, and Amber laughed.

"Timing," she said.

"I *wish* my love life was that exciting."

"Give."

"Marcy Richards," he said.

"She is?"

His memory was warm. "My high school sweetheart. Tall, lanky, long red hair, a few freckles. She was captain of the girls' basketball team."

"What happened?"

"Tragic story, really. Senior year, she met a guy from Skagway. He was in town for a tournament. He kissed her. I punched him. She cried. But then four months later they both went off to U of Alaska. They're married now with two kids."

"Do you miss her?"

"Not really. She's my accountant, so I see her every week. She's great. And so, it turns out, is her husband, Mike."

"You're saying you're over the heartbreak?"

"I went off to flight school and had a series of short but satisfying relationships. Turns out, women can't resist a pilot."

"How short?"

"Hours, sometimes days."

"That's appalling."

"I was recovering from heartbreak. I was young and vulnerable."

"*Vulnerable* isn't the word I'd use."

He grinned. "You'd be right."

"And now?" she asked, brandishing her nearly empty mug.

"A few dates here and there, nothing that's ever turned into anything but a friendship. I'm pretty busy with Aviation 58, and Juneau's population is not that huge. A lot of the women my age have moved on."

"You ever think about moving on?" she asked.

He shook his head. "I love it there. And given how much Aviation 58 has grown, my roots are pretty deep."

"Maybe you can find a nice girl in Atlanta and take her home with you." There was a glow in her blue eyes that seemed to reach right down to his soul.

"Good idea. You doing anything for the next thirty or forty years?"

She set down the empty mug. "I know you're joking, but that's a pretty good line."

He wished he was certain it was a line. He pointed to her mug. "You want another?"

"I need to get home so Isabel can leave."

Six

As Isabel left the penthouse, Amber made her way down the hall to where Cole had gone in search of Otis. The dog had apparently plunked himself down in Zachary's open doorway and gone to sleep.

She found Otis there, with Cole inside the bedroom, tucking a blanket over the sleeping Zachary. Cole rubbed a gentle hand across Zachary's forehead before turning away from the crib. In the doorway, Amber stood to one side, her chest strangely warm.

"Sound asleep," Cole whispered as he stepped over Otis.

The dog opened one eye but didn't lift his head.

"Isabel said he slept right through," Amber whispered in return.

"Good for him." Cole stopped right in front of her.

He was close, too close, but she didn't want to move. Instead, she inhaled deeply, letting his fresh, masculine scent fill her lungs. It was a fight to keep from reaching out to touch him.

"Hi," he breathed.

She lifted her chin to gaze up at him, wishing he would kiss her, but knowing any more intimacy was a very bad idea. Her life was complicated, and he was leaving, and she needed to keep her focus on the court case. But the temptation to lean into his arms and forget everything for just a little while was almost overwhelming.

He brought his palm to her cheek, and the warmth of the contact seemed to flow through her entire body. Her breasts tingled and she parted her lips, subconsciously inching toward him.

His free arm slipped around her waist, and he slowly dipped his head to meet hers. "Is this just a kiss good-night?"

"I don't know." She grasped the sleeves of his shirt, anchoring herself.

"Fair enough." His soft lips captured hers.

His kiss was everything she remembered and more. It was

more than his lips, more than his tongue, more than his taste. Every pore on her body drank in his essence. Her heart rate increased. Her blood heated. She pressed herself against him, nipples beading against his hard chest, thighs molding to his, hands twining around his neck, into his hair then back again, tracing the planes and angles of his face.

She wanted to memorize his skin. She wanted to touch him everywhere, imprint every contour onto her brain.

Arousal swiftly pushed away reason.

Needing to get closer still, she worked her hands between them, struggling in the tight space to release the buttons on his shirt. In answer, his hands slid down her back, across her waist, cupping her rear, pulling her tight against his body, letting her know how strongly he desired her.

She stripped off her sweater. Her tank top followed. And she was before him in a white lacy bra.

He drew back and his pupils dilated, his breathing labored. He swore under his breath, then stripped off his shirt and backed her tight against the cool wall. He lifted her there, bringing her legs around his waist.

He flicked the catch on her bra, pulling it from between them, and they were skin to skin. She was in heaven.

His voice was a rumble against her mouth. "Amber?"

It was a struggle to speak. "Yes?"

"This is more than just a good-night kiss."

"Yes," she rasped. "Yes."

He worked his way down her neck, kissing the curve of her shoulder, then the swell of her breast. His lips fastened onto her nipple, and her body bucked, fingertips curling hard into his muscular shoulders. He switched sides, and her head tipped back, legs going tight around him.

"Which way?" he asked.

"Left," she rasped. "My left. End of the hall."

He scooped her into his arms and paced to the bedroom door, pushing it open and crossing to the big bed.

There he tossed back the covers and set her down. In a split second, he was with her, covering her body with his, kissing her deeply, his hands roaming her skin.

She went on an exploration of her own, following the hard definition of his shoulders and biceps, to his pecs and his washboard stomach. She unsnapped his jeans. He immediately did the same.

Then he pulled back to look into her eyes.

Without a word, he dragged down her zipper.

She followed suit, the backs of her knuckles grazing him as she went.

He sucked in a tight breath, eyes as dark as coal while they watched her.

She tugged down his jeans, and he kicked them off.

He pulled off her pants, palms skimming across her silk panties, back and forth, until she twitched in reaction. She moaned his name.

He kissed her breasts, and her arms stretched out, hands clenching into fists. And then her panties were gone. His boxers disappeared, and he had a condom. Thank goodness he had a condom.

He was on top of her, pressing into her, so slowly, so exquisitely. She arched against him, wrapping her arms and legs around him. She'd never felt anything that came close to Cole Parker.

He smelled of fresh air and wide-open spaces. He tasted like chocolate and brandy. His callused fingertips were rough and hot as he caressed every intimate spot on her skin. His body was shifting iron beneath her hands.

His weight felt good. His thrusts were focused, and her body reflexively adjusted its angle to accommodate him. He whispered her name. Then his arm braced the small of her back, pressing them tighter and tighter together.

Everything else was forgotten except the sensations cresting endlessly through her body as she climbed higher and higher. Colors glowed behind her eyes while white noise roared in her ears. Her world contracted to their joined bodies, tighter and tighter, until the dam exploded. The colors turned to fireworks, and sound boomed like a symphony as Cole called out her name.

Her pulse was in overdrive, and she was dragging in oxygen. Her limbs lost all feeling as she sank deeper and deeper into the soft mattress.

"You still with me?" Cole asked from what seemed like a distance.

"I think so. I'm not sure. Are we in Kansas?"

He chuckled. "I was *definitely* over the rainbow."

Reality floated its way back. "Oh, my."

"Don't second-guess," he warned.

"That was a lot more than just a kiss."

He brushed back her hair and looked into her eyes. "It felt kind of inevitable."

She knew what he meant. Every second they spent together seemed to draw them closer and closer.

"Maybe it was good to get it over with," she ventured.

"At least we're not wondering anymore."

"Were you?" she couldn't help asking. "Were you wondering?"

"Absolutely. From the first second I laid eyes on you. That's why I botched it so bad that night at the dance."

"It was a rocky start," she agreed. "But you rescued me. Then you rescued my shoes."

"You hate those shoes."

"True. But you do get points for trying."

He skimmed the backs of his fingers along her side. "Are those points redeemable?"

His touch was distracting, and his eyes were taking on that dark glow again.

"For valuable prizes," she told him.

He traced the curve of her hip. "What do I get?"

"What do you want?"

He seemed to hesitate for a moment. "To stay."

A shimmer of anticipation warmed her chest at the thought of sleeping in Cole's arms, waking up next to him, having breakfast together with Zachary.

"Are you serious?"

"Absolutely."

"Okay."

Cole awoke to the feel of Amber spooned in his arms and the realization that he had to tell her the truth. Up until last night, he'd been prepared to breeze into town, make sure Zachary was settled and breeze back out again. But things had changed. She had changed them.

She rolled onto her back, blinking her eyes in the dim light from the window.

"Morning," he said softly.

A pretty smile grew on her face. "Morning."

Otis whimpered at the door.

Then Zachary let out a cry down the hall.

"Is Isabel in yet?" Cole asked.

Amber craned her neck to look at the bedside clock. "Not for an hour."

Otis whined more insistently and Zachary's cries grew steady.

Cole grimaced. "I'll walk the dog if you feed the baby."

"Sorry," said Amber.

"Not your fault at all." He sat up, shaking off sleep. "We jumped from a one-night stand to an old married couple in the blink of an eye."

"Not the morning you had in mind," she asked from behind him.

He turned, already smiling. "Oddly, it feels like the perfect morning. Shall I pick up some bagels while I'm out?"

She rose from the other side of the bed, gloriously naked and indescribably beautiful. "Make mine blueberry."

"You got it." He forced himself to look away and pulled on his jeans.

Otis's leash was at the front door, along with Cole's jacket. They took the elevator, and once they were on the sidewalk, they headed to the park.

Cole let the fresh air clear his brain. While they walked, he

formulated and discarded several versions of a speech to Amber.
Should he plunge in with the fact that he was Samuel's long-lost
son? Or should he go about it chronologically, outline his mo-
tivation and rationale before hitting her with his real identity?

He didn't want to upset her. He didn't want to worry her. And
he certainly didn't want to make her distrust or dislike him any
more than he already had. But last night had been too amazing
for anything less than complete honesty.

He and Otis ended up on the opposite side of the park. They
made their way down the block to a bakery Cole had found a
couple of days ago. He left Otis outside and chose a variety of
bagels, then they started back to the penthouse.

He found himself wondering what Zachary ate. Would he
like to try a bit of bagel? Or did he stick to pureed foods?

Cole knew absolutely nothing about babies or toddlers. All
he knew was that Zachary was adorable, and that he was curious about the stages of development to come. He hoped once
he told Amber the truth, she'd be willing to send him pictures
and videos. Maybe he could even come back occasionally and
check up on Zachary.

The more he thought about it, the more he realized acknowledging their blood relationship was the right thing to do. He
wasn't sure why he waited so long.

Nearly an hour had gone by before he returned to the penthouse. Amber had given him her spare key, so he let himself
in, wondering if Zachary would have finished his bottle and
might be having a morning bath. He hoped he wasn't being
fussy for Amber.

When Cole opened the door, he did hear Zachary's cries.
But they were interspersed with adult voices. At first he assumed Isabel had arrived. But it was a man speaking, then another answering.

Cole and Otis rounded the corner to the living room to see
Roth Calvin and four other men standing with Amber in the
middle of the room. Two of the men were on cell phones, while
Amber was holding a crying Zachary. Cole reflexively moved
forward to take the baby.

"What's going on?" he asked, worried that something had gone wrong in the court battle.

"Thank you," whispered Amber as Zachary's cries quieted. "Isabel's running late, and we've got a problem."

Cole glanced at the other four men. "What's wrong?"

"A Coast Eagle flight is in trouble," said one of them.

Cole went instantly on alert. "What kind of trouble?"

"Hydraulic failure," said the shortest of the three. "The landing gear won't come down."

"What's he doing here?" Roth demanded, ending his call, seeming to have just recognized Cole.

"I brought bagels," said Cole.

"Zachary likes him," said Amber.

"What kind of plane?" Cole asked.

"We've got work to do here," said a large, rotund, fiftysomething man with gray hair and a bulbous nose.

"Cole," said Amber. "This is Max Cutter. He's our interim president. This is Sidney Raines and Julius Fonteno, both vice presidents. You know Roth."

"What kind of plane?" Cole repeated. The size of the plane dictated the scale of the problem.

Julius, the large man, frowned. "Shouldn't you go change a diaper or something?"

Cole braced his feet apart. "It'll be faster if you just answer the question."

"Boonsome 300 over LAX," said Sidney, the shorter, younger man, glancing up from the screen of his phone. "They're reporting twenty minutes of fuel left."

Cole's stomach sank. A Boonsome 300 was a passenger jet. There were up to two hundred souls on board.

Max Cutter ended his own call. "The pilot's leaving the holding pattern and bringing her in."

Cole looked to Amber. She was still and pale.

"Are you a pilot?" he asked Sidney.

"Yes."

"They've checked the pump circuit breakers?" Cole knew

the answer would be yes. But he couldn't help going through the diagnostics in his mind.

Sidney gave a nod.

"Any visible leaks?"

"None," said Sidney. "Foam's down on the runway."

"They'll cycle the gear again?"

"They will."

Cole stepped closer to Amber, wishing he could reach out and take her hand. A belly landing in a plane that size was incredibly risky.

"Gear's down," said Sidney, grasping the back of the sofa even as he uttered the words. "They cycled the gear one last time. They've got hydraulic pressure back."

Relief rushed through Cole.

Amber dropped into an armchair, a slight tremor in her hands. "Thank goodness."

"They're on short final," said Sidney, putting his phone to his ear. "Tower's patched me in."

They all waited, watching Sidney closely until he gave the thumbs-up. "Wheels down. It's all good."

"Yes," hissed Max.

"Relief valve, do you think?" Cole posed the question to Sidney.

"They'll have to go through the whole system."

Roth spoke up. "Amber, get the communications director on the phone."

Cole bristled at Roth's abrupt tone, but Amber moved to the landline.

Roth continued talking. "We'll call it a minor delay in the deployment of the landing gear. All safety procedures were followed, and it was an isolated incident."

Amber stopped, looking back over her shoulder. "An isolated incident?"

"Yes."

"We know this how?"

"Because we've been flying the Boonsomes for nearly ten years, and it's never happened before."

"I don't like the word *isolated*," said Amber.

Roth's eyes narrowed.

"I'd suggest replacing that clause with everyone on board is safe, and there were no injuries. Once we've confirmed that's the case."

Roth squared his shoulders. "The whole point of a press release is to reassure the public—"

"I agree with Amber," said Max.

"Of *course* you agree with Amber," said Roth. "You're her appointee."

"I agree with Amber, too," said Sidney.

Roth set his jaw.

"I have to side with Roth on this," said Julius. "The more reassurance we can give our passengers, the better."

"It's early days," said Cole. "Better to mitigate your words until the investigation is complete."

"Who let this guy in here?" asked Julius.

"I'm an airline pilot," said Cole. He might not be a Coast Airlines employee, but he knew the industry.

"Bully for you," said Julius.

"It might be better if you excused us," Roth said to Cole.

Cole looked to Amber. He could go or he could stay, but he was taking his cue from her, not from Roth.

"What about the other Boonsome 300s in service?" asked Max. He was scrolling through the screen on his phone. "Here. Midpoint Airlines just grounded theirs."

"That was fast," said Sidney.

"Kneejerk," said Julius. "It's not like there's a pattern."

"They've got a total of three Boonsomes," said Roth. "It's an easy decision for them to make."

"It puts pressure on us," said Sidney.

"We're not caving to pressure," said Roth. "We've got twenty-four Boonsomes. It's a quarter of our fleet."

Amber's hand was resting on the telephone. "We could have lost two hundred passengers."

"We didn't," said Julius.

"We're *not* considering this," said Roth with finality. "Unless the federal regulator orders us, we are *not* grounding twenty-four airplanes."

"It's a publicity grab from Midpoint," said Julius.

Cole couldn't help jumping in. "Depending on the problem."

"We'll find the problem," said Roth. "And we'll fix it. Nobody's suggesting we send that particular plane up again without a thorough overhaul."

"And if something happens with another Boonsome?" asked Sidney.

"Nothing's going to happen," said Roth.

"You're playing the odds," said Amber.

"I play the odds every time I get out of bed," said Roth. "You want one hundred percent certainty? We lose a million dollars a day with those planes on the ground. *That's* a certainty. It'll take two weeks minimum to get any answers on an investigation. Anybody want to do the math?"

Max looked to Amber. "What are your thoughts?"

"That's a lot of money," she said. "But it's a lot of lives to risk, too." Her gaze moved to Cole.

Julius gestured to Amber, disdain in his tone. "*This* is our leader?"

"She's looking for input," said Max. "I'm looking for input, too."

Roth's face twisted into a sneer. "My input is don't bankrupt the company while you're temporarily in charge."

Cole clamped his jaw to stop himself from speaking.

"The plane is at the gate," said Sidney. "And the terminal is full of reporters."

"We have to put out a statement," said Roth.

"We have to make a decision," Amber told him.

"We don't have a choice," said Julius. "Nobody's giving up a million dollars a day."

"Say that again after we lose a plane full of passengers," said Sidney.

"Do you want my opinion?" Cole asked Amber.

"Yes."

Roth let out an inarticulate exclamation.

Cole ignored him. "Ask yourself this. Before the inspectors identify the problem, would you risk putting Zachary on a Boonsome 300?"

Amber shook her head.

"We ground the planes," said Max.

"Have you *lost your minds?*" asked Julius.

Amber squared her shoulders and gave Max a sharp nod of agreement.

Pride swelled up inside Cole's chest.

"This is amateur hour," Roth spat. "Believe me, you haven't heard the last of it."

"We'll request an expedited investigation," said Max. "But for now the decision is final."

Amber focused in on Cole, moving closer to speak in an undertone. "I have to go to the office."

"I know." He realized their conversation about Samuel would have to wait.

"Can you stay with Zachary until Isabel gets here? She thought maybe noon."

"Don't worry, I'll stay."

Relief flooded her eyes. "Thank you."

"No problem. Talk to you later?"

"I'll call you."

"Good luck."

"Everyone's safe. That's a whole lot of luck already."

The group moved toward the door, Amber grabbing her purse and throwing a coat over her slacks and sweater. When the last of them left and the door latched shut, Cole turned his attention to Zachary.

The baby was sucking on the sleeve of his stretchy one-piece suit.

"You like bagels?" Cole asked.

"Gak baw," said Zachary, grabbing at Cole's nose.

Amber's day went from frightening to stressful to downright infuriating. At six o'clock, Destiny was sitting across from her at her compact office meeting table.

"*That's* how Roth spent his day?" she asked Destiny.

Destiny pushed a sheaf of papers across the table. "I don't know how they did it, but they got an emergency court date. The custody hearing starts at nine tomorrow morning."

"I thought we'd have weeks to get ready." Amber gave the paperwork a passing glance, but she trusted Destiny's assessment.

"We have hours to get ready."

"Can we do it?"

"Not as well as I'd like. But we can work hard tonight. And Roth's side is under the same deadline."

Amber's cell phone rang.

"Remember," said Destiny, "the fundamentals remain the same. Coco's codicil is legal and valid. They have to prove you're not a fit guardian."

Amber didn't recognize the calling number. "Hello?"

"Amber, it's Cole."

She glanced to Destiny, feeling a small spike of guilt about last night. "Hi, Cole."

Destiny's interest obviously perked up.

"I need to talk to you about something."

"Is it Zachary?"

"No, no. He's fine. At least, he was fine when I left him with Isabel this afternoon. Can you meet me for dinner?"

She wished she could. "I'm afraid not. Destiny and I are going to be busy."

There was silence on his end. "It's kind of important."

"I'm sorry."

"Maybe later?"

"Tonight's not going to be good. We'll be working really late."

"Is everything okay?"

"Yes." She hesitated. "No." She knew she shouldn't share, since she barely knew him. But she felt like she owed him an explanation. "It's actually not okay. Roth's convinced the judge to hold an emergency hearing tomorrow morning. He's going after custody."

"Tomorrow morning?"

"He's going to use my decision on the Boonsome 300s as proof I'm unfit to control Coast Eagle."

"He'll lose, Amber."

"I hope so." Her stomach was already beginning to cramp up. "Is there anything I can do?"

"Ask me out again in a few days?"

Destiny's brows went up.

"Happy to," he answered. Then his tone changed. "I really wish I could see you now. Even for a short time."

"That would be nice. But we're pretty much pulling an all-nighter here. I'm about to call Isabel and arrange for her to stay over."

"I could stay at your place, wait for you there."

"Not necessary." She wasn't going to let herself presume any more on Cole's good graces. He didn't come to Atlanta to be a babysitter.

He was quiet again. Then he blew out a breath. "Okay. A couple of days, then."

"Thanks."

"Nothing to thank me for. Good luck."

"Thanks for that." She'd take every scrap of luck she could get. "Bye, Cole."

"Bye."

She pressed the end button and set down the phone.

Destiny spoke. "We're going to take thirty seconds of our valuable time here, and you're going to tell me what's going on with Cole. Then I'm putting it completely out of my mind until after the hearing." She glanced at her watch. "Go."

"I like him. He likes me. We went skating last night, then we drank killer hot chocolate. We went back to my place, slept together, which was pretty killer, too. Then he stayed over, went out for bagels and then all hell broke loose. He wanted to see me again tonight, but…" She spread her arms.

"Holy cow," said Destiny in obvious awe. "We are definitely going to talk more about this. But right now we've got a whole lot of work to do."

Seven

Cole and Luca slipped into the back of the courtroom. Word had obviously gotten out about the hearing, because the room was packed with reporters and onlookers. He couldn't help but feel bad for Amber. It was stressful enough to have Zachary's custody on the line without an audience of one hundred.

Predictably, Roth's side attacked Coco. They started by disparaging her motivations in marrying an older, wealthy man, then they called witness after witness, painting an unflattering picture of her intellect. Cole knew from conversations with Amber that Coco was emotional and sometimes erratic, but the witnesses made her sound unstable, unprincipled, even dishonest.

Luca tipped his head closer to Cole. "How much do you think is true?"

"She did marry a billionaire nearly three times her age. And I don't think she was a rocket scientist."

Cole imagined a lot of what was being said about Coco's temper and her behavior at parties was accurate. Then again, if she'd been at a frat party like most nineteen-year-olds, instead of at a posh charity function or the opening of an art museum, nobody would have raised an eyebrow.

"Doesn't mean she wasn't a good mother," said Luca.

"And it doesn't mean her wishes shouldn't be respected." Nothing Cole had heard so far would indicate mental incompetence on the part of Coco.

Roth took the stand, and the gallery's attention seemed to heighten. Cole guessed most people here knew the pivotal players in the drama.

Roth's own lawyer questioned him first.

"Did you and Samuel Henderson ever discuss his future plans for Coast Eagle Airlines?" the lawyer asked.

"Extensively and on many occasions," Roth answered.

"Did he ask your advice?"

"Yes, he did."

"To your knowledge, did he ever ask his wife, Coco Henderson's, advice on Coast Eagle Airlines?"

Roth smirked. "Never."

"You're certain?"

"Positive."

"Objection," said Destiny.

"Sustained," said the judge.

"I'll rephrase," said the lawyer. "Did Samuel ever say anything directly to you regarding his opinion of his wife's advice on Coast Eagle?"

"He told me she knew nothing about business. He said he never discussed it with her."

The lawyer gave a satisfied nod. "Did Samuel Henderson indicate to you that he wanted his son to one day take over the business?"

"Yes. Samuel loved his son deeply. I've never seen him so happy as when Zachary was born. He talked about keeping the airline in the family for another generation. It was his fondest wish that Coast Eagle be protected and preserved for his son."

Destiny rose again. "Objection. The witness is not in a position to know Samuel Henderson's fondest wish."

"That's what he said to me," said Roth.

"Overruled," said the judge.

"Did Samuel ever speak to you about his wife having any kind of a hand in running Coast Eagle Airlines in the event of his death?"

"He did," said Roth, and an odd expression flicked in his eyes.

Cole found himself doubting Roth's honesty on the question.

Roth answered, "He said the only people he trusted with Coast Eagle and with his son were Dryden Dunsmore and me. He said someone needed to control Coco because she had the decision-making ability of a twelve-year-old."

"He said that directly to you? Those were his words?"

"Yes. And they're supported by his will, which included

both Dryden and I in guardianship or controlling positions in Coast Eagle."

"A little too convenient," Cole whispered to Luca.

"I can't tell if the judge is buying it or not."

Destiny cross-examined but wasn't able to poke holes in Roth's story. Cole and Luca slipped out at the lunch break, picking a restaurant several blocks away to avoid being seen by Amber or Destiny. By late afternoon, Amber was the only witness left.

Roth's lawyer started with Amber's competence at Coast Eagle. It went as expected. There was no getting around her lack of experience, but Cole thought she held her own, particularly on yesterday's decision to ground the Boonsome jets. Yes, it was a financial loss, but risking passenger lives was too dangerous.

Unfortunately, it then came to light that their closest competitor had not grounded their Boonsomes, and Amber's decision had, at least in the short term, put Coast Eagle at a competitive disadvantage. The lawyers successfully framed her decision as emotional and even brought Cole into the equation, accusing Amber of taking advice from a competitor on a confidential corporate matter.

It wasn't going well for Amber's side.

"You were ten years older than your stepsister?" the lawyer then asked her.

The question obviously surprised Amber, and it seemed to take her a moment to regroup. "Yes."

"And you left home when she was eight years old?"

"I did."

"How often did you see her after that?"

"Not often."

"Once a week, once a month, once a year?"

"Maybe once a year," Amber admitted, causing a small flurry of whispers in the courtroom.

"Until you introduced her to Samuel Henderson."

"Yes," said Amber.

"And why did you introduce them to each other?"

"Coco was in town. When I mentioned the corporate Christmas party at Coast Eagle, she asked to go with me."

"She asked to go with you?"

"Coco enjoyed parties."

"Yes, I think we've established that already."

"Objection," said Destiny.

"I withdraw the comment," said the lawyer. "After she began dating Samuel Henderson, would you say you and your stepsister grew closer?"

"We did."

"And you saw each other how often then?"

"A couple of times a month. She was busy. And she was newly married. And she had a lot of obligations."

Cole wanted to tell Amber to stop talking. She was sounding defensive, as if she was embarrassed that they weren't closer.

"Tell me, Ms. Welsley, how did Coco feel about her baby?"

"She loved Zachary very much."

"As mothers do."

Amber didn't answer.

Cole applauded that decision.

"What about before he was born?"

She went still, and her face paled a shade. "I don't understand."

"I don't like this," Cole muttered beneath his breath. Something was clearly wrong.

"Before Zachary was born. How did Coco feel about being pregnant?"

"She was healthy. There were no particular problems, morning sickness or anything."

"I'm not talking about her physical health, Ms. Welsley. I'm talking about her emotional health."

Again, Amber stayed silent.

"Was your stepsister happy to be pregnant with Zachary?"

Cole got a cold feeling in the pit of his stomach.

"She was surprised," said Amber. "She hadn't planned on it happening so soon."

"Surprised or upset?"

Amber paused. "She was upset at first."

"Upset enough to get an abortion?"

Amber's hesitation said it all.

"Damn it," Cole ground out.

"She didn't get an abortion," said Amber.

"Did she want an abortion?"

"Objection," said Destiny.

"I'll rephrase," said the lawyer. "Did she ever tell you she wanted an abortion?"

The silence was unfortunately long.

"Once," Amber admitted.

"Did you talk her out of getting an abortion?"

"I gave her my opinion."

"Which was?"

"That babies were always good news. And that she was going to be a wonderful mother."

"Is it fair to say you changed her mind?"

Amber didn't answer.

"Ms. Welsley? Is it fair to say you changed your stepsister's mind, talked her out of getting the abortion she desired?"

"She wasn't serious," said Amber. "She was upset. She was newly married, and being pregnant came as a shock to her."

"Did she make an appointment at an abortion clinic?"

"No."

The lawyer waited.

"She didn't."

"Perhaps not to the best of your knowledge. But I can tell you she *did* make an appointment at an abortion clinic."

A collective gasp went up in the gallery, followed by whispered comments.

The judge pounded his gavel, and the room returned to quiet.

The lawyer returned to his table, lifting a piece of paper with a flourish. "I have here a copy of an appointment card for Coco Henderson for the Women's Central Health Clinic."

"Where did you get that?"

"From the Women's Central Health Clinic."

"Coco obviously did not have an abortion."

"Because you talked her out of it. Like so many of your step-sister's childish, ill-informed impulses, had you not been there to persuade her otherwise, the consequences would have been catastrophic. She would have had an abortion, and Zachary would never have been born."

The sick feeling of defeat was written across Amber's face. Cole fought an urge to go to her. He wanted to pull her into his arms and tell her everything was going to be okay. But he couldn't. And it wasn't.

"That was a body blow," said Luca.

There was nothing Destiny could do to counter the revelations. Both lawyers walked through closing arguments, but there wasn't a single person in the room who trusted Coco's judgment, nor was there anyone who truly believed she had her son's best interests at heart.

Samuel had been shown to be a loving father, thrilled from minute one that they were expecting a baby. Coco looked selfish and petulant, her intelligence and judgment suspect.

Destiny sat down and put an arm around Amber's shoulders.

"You have to do it," Luca whispered.

"Do what?"

"Tell them who you are."

Cole shot Luca a look of astonishment. *"What?"*

"Now. Right now. Put in a bid for custody. You're a blood relative."

"Custody?" Had Luca lost his mind?

"At the very least, it'll throw a wrench in it, slow things down. If you don't, if the judge rules on this—and it looks like he's about to rule—then it's done."

Adrenaline shot into Cole's system, and his stomach clenched. How could he do it? How could he not?

"Ms. Welsley," said the judge, "I have no doubt as to the love you feel for Zachary. However—"

"Do it!" Luca hissed.

Cole shot to his feet. "Your Honor."

The judge drew back in obvious shock. "You're out of order, sir."

"Go, go, go," said Luca.

Cole moved into the aisle and walked forward.

Amber and Destiny both turned to stare. But he didn't dare look at them.

"Bailiff," called the judge.

Cole knew he had only seconds. "My name is Cole Parker Henderson. I'm Samuel Henderson's son."

Amber felt her world dissolve beneath her.

Cole continued walking to the front of the courtroom. He continued talking. He didn't even bother to look her way.

"I want to petition the court for custody of my half brother," his voice boomed.

"He's a competitor," Roth cried out, coming to his feet.

"Order," called the judge, bringing down his gavel.

The bailiff seemed uncertain of what to do.

Destiny whispered in an undertone, "What the—?"

"I'm *such* an idiot," said Amber.

"Can it possibly be true?"

Cole came to a stop at the little gateway.

Amber took in Cole's expression. "That's no bluff."

He was firm and resolute. She realized he had to have planned this all along. And she'd let him in. She'd trusted him. She'd armed him with all kinds of information. She'd left him alone in the penthouse, alone with Zachary.

"This is preposterous," said Roth. "It's a stalling tactic."

Cole glared at him. "It's easy enough to prove. DNA, for example."

"That'll take time. And we're losing money by the hour. Your Honor, this can't possibly be legal."

Roth's lawyer stood. "Your Honor, you were about to rule."

A voice came from the back of the room. "We have a DNA test."

Cole spun.

Luca came to his feet. "Your Honor, I have the results of a DNA test by Central Laboratories, proving Samuel's paternity."

"What do we do?" asked Amber, panic beginning to build deep in her stomach.

"Wait," said Destiny, watching the judge closely.

The judge finally spoke. "I'm not persuaded that a genetic relationship alone alters the merits of this case. Samuel Henderson could have any number of illegitimate children—"

"They were married," Cole's deep voice intoned.

Silence followed the pronouncement.

"My mother and Samuel Henderson were married." He shot a sharp look to Roth. "Again, very easy to prove."

Luca spoke. "I have a copy of the marriage certificate and the divorce decree."

Cole turned to stare at Luca for a long moment.

Destiny leaned close to Amber. "*This* is a whole new ballgame. Hang tough."

Destiny came sharply to her feet. "Your Honor, we ask for a recess."

Roth's lawyer jumped in. "*We* ask for a ruling."

But Destiny wasn't finished. "Under the terms of the will, as a legitimate child of Samuel Henderson, Cole Henderson is entitled to half of Samuel's estate."

The courtroom erupted.

"Order, order," the judge called over the din. "Court is in recess until such time as Samuel Henderson's will can be reviewed." He looked to Cole. "Mr. Henderson, if you do not already have a lawyer, I suggest you get one."

Everybody left their seats, and the courtroom turned into a mob scene. Cole stood still, the crowd jostling around him. He was nearly chest to chest with the bailiff guarding the low gate.

"Get me out of here," Amber said to Destiny. "I can't see him. I can't talk to him."

"We can take the side door." Destiny grabbed her briefcase.

All Amber wanted to do was get back to Zachary. For a horrible moment there, she'd known she was about to lose him. Zachary had almost been ripped from her care and given over to Roth. She was still shaking with reaction.

"Amber," called Cole.

She refused to look at him. "Go away."

"I wanted to tell you. I tried to tell you."

She let out a short, high-pitched laugh. "When? *When?* It's not like you lacked opportunity."

"We need to talk."

"We've talked enough. I've told you enough." She turned away.

"Amber," Cole tried again.

Luca's voice interrupted. "Destiny, we need a copy of the will."

"Not *now*," said Cole.

Destiny's tone was sharp. "As if you haven't already read it."

"We haven't," said Luca.

"Why the theatrics?"

"You were about to lose," said Luca.

"Amber?" Cole tried again.

Destiny appealed to Cole. "This is not a good time."

"I don't particularly care. You can't ignore this."

Amber glared at him. She wanted to yell at him. He'd deceived her. He'd slept with her. He'd let her think he cared about Zachary.

But before she could do anything stupid, she forced herself to turn and walk away.

She left the courtroom and all but ran down the hallway to the foyer. It was full of reporters, but she ignored their questions. She ignored everything, striding blindly for the exit.

Destiny caught up. "You're doing great. Just keep walking. My car's to the left, one block up."

"I remember. I need to see Zachary."

"We'll go there first."

"Ms. Welsley, did you have any idea Samuel had another son?"

"Did your sister know Samuel had another wife?"

"Did Coco have any other abortions?"

Destiny hit the unlock button and pulled open the passenger door for Amber. Amber climbed inside and slammed the door, not particularly caring if she smashed someone's camera.

And then Destiny was inside, too. She started the car, and the reporters finally backed off.

"You okay?" she asked, reaching out to touch Amber's shoulder.

"I'm terrible," Amber answered.

She felt trapped, desperate. For a wild moment, she thought about sneaking Zachary out of the country, hiding out on a beach somewhere where nobody could find them.

"What happens now?" she asked, her voice shaking.

"First, we comb through the will."

"Does Cole really get half?"

"Unless there's something I'm remembering wrong, yes, he does."

Amber's voice broke over the next question. "Will he get Zachary?"

"I don't know, honey. I honestly don't know."

Amber's mind scrambled, zipping from Zachary to Coast Eagle, to the Boonsome 300, and then to Cole.

"I have to talk to Max," she told Destiny. "I have to get back to the office."

"Do you want to go home first?"

Amber shook her head. "I'll call Isabel. Roth will go straight to Coast Eagle, and who knows what move he'll try to make next." She realized in a rush that despite everything, she feared Roth more than she feared Cole.

Back at the office, Roth had fought with Max. Julius had argued with Sidney. Each of the board members had called to express their concern. Though, thankfully, all had agreed that Max should stay in place for now as interim president.

Destiny had reviewed Samuel's will and was now on her way to the penthouse to meet Amber. It was nearly ten by the time Amber finally made it through the door, exhausted and starving.

She kicked off her shoes, shrugged out of her steel-gray blazer and dumped her purse on a table in the living room. Destiny had promised to bring a large pepperoni and mushroom, while Amber was in charge of margaritas.

She called out to Isabel, then, without stopping, she went directly to the kitchen and dumped a tray of ice cubes, lime juice, tequila and orange liqueur into the blender and set it on high.

The doorbell rang, and she padded through the living room to greet Destiny.

"Extra cheese?" she asked hopefully as she eyed the large cardboard carton.

"You bet."

"Come on in."

While Destiny settled the pizza on the kitchen island and retrieved the plates, Amber poured the margaritas into two large glasses.

"I've been seriously thinking about strapping Zachary into his car seat and heading for the border," said Amber.

"Which border?"

"Does it matter? I can't help but think we'd be better off if nobody could find us."

"You might be better off, but I'd have a legal nightmare to unravel."

"I suppose."

The fight suddenly went out of Amber, and exhaustion set in. She climbed onto one of the stools and helped herself to a slice of the gooey pizza.

"You could try to make a deal with Cole," Destiny suggested. She started with a sip of the slushy drink. "It's pretty clear he's after Coast Eagle."

"Do you think Samuel knew about him?" In her few spare moments this evening, Amber couldn't help but wonder if Samuel had shunned Cole and kept him a secret or had been oblivious to his existence.

"Interesting wording in the will," said Destiny. "Either Samuel knew, or at least suspected he had a child with his first wife, or he was planning more children with Coco."

"He definitely wanted more children," said Amber.

There was more silence.

"An abortion?" asked Destiny.

"I almost couldn't talk her out of it."

"For future reference, that's the kind of thing you want to share with your lawyer."

"I had no idea it would ever come out."

"Everything always comes out eventually."

"I didn't know she'd made an appointment. She didn't tell me that. It was one night—one long, horrible night where we argued. And then she changed her mind. I don't remember any of the staff being around. I thought nobody knew but me."

"She might have told Samuel."

Amber gave her head a decisive shake. "She knew how much he wanted children. If she'd had an abortion, it would have been in secret. She'd never have admitted to him she'd had doubts."

They both fell silent, chewing their way through the pizza slices.

"We were about to lose, weren't we?" Amber asked.

"We were about to lose big-time. Roth knows how to run Coast Eagle, and Samuel was way out front in the character debate."

"Just because Coco was self-centered doesn't mean she was wrong to choose me."

"I agree," said Destiny, helping herself to another slice. "We need to figure out Cole's plan. I can guess at Roth's next move. Between Samuel and his mother, the Hendersons controlled sixty-five percent of Coast Eagle. The other shareholders are minor, mostly companies, none with more than seven percent. But Roth still has a play. If he gets custody, therefore half of the Henderson family shares, and if he can bring the other shareholders on side, he'll control the board and get himself appointed as president."

"He doesn't care anything about Zachary."

"True, but all but impossible to prove," said Destiny. "Samuel named him guardian for some reason."

"If Cole gets custody, he controls all sixty-five percent. He's invincible." Amber paused. "But why the ruse?"

"He was obviously looking for information, solidifying his position. That has to be why Luca was cozying up to me."

"Did you tell Luca anything?"

"Nothing that wasn't already public. Cole obviously saw you as his primary rival rather than Ross. I'm guessing he was either going to co-opt you or take you out."

"He must have been shocked when it went in Roth's favor."

"And had to suddenly change the game plan. I don't think they planned it like that."

"They did have DNA and a marriage certificate at the ready."

"True," said Destiny.

Amber took a drink, appreciating the hit of alcohol warming her system. "What do we do now?"

"We need more information on Cole."

"Maybe I could seduce it out of him. No, wait. I already tried that."

Destiny gazed at her for a moment, the tone of her voice going softer. "How was it?"

"Seriously?"

Destiny gave a helpless shrug. "What can it hurt to tell me now?"

Amber set down her half-eaten slice of pizza, regret enveloping her. "It was great. He was funny, romantic, totally into me." She swiped back her hair. "At least he seemed totally into me. Too bad he was faking the whole thing." Every time she thought about their night together, the humiliation returned. "I'm not sure I can face him again."

"I could talk to Luca instead. He might give me something we can use."

"Did you sleep with Luca?"

"Almost. He tried pretty hard."

Amber held up her glass in a toast. "You're a stronger woman than me. And you've still got that as leverage."

"I'd have said yes eventually."

"But you won't anymore, right?"

"I won't anymore," said Destiny. "Well, unless I think it'll make him talk. Then, well, okay, I'd be willing to take one for the team."

Eight

"I know she's here," Cole said to Luca as he pulled open the steel door of the Coast Eagle hangar. "And she'll have to be polite."

He knew Amber wouldn't dare step out of line at the Coast Eagle children's Christmas party. She'd have to listen to him.

He walked inside.

Carols chimed from unseen speakers, while soap bubbles drifted around them like snow. White lights and colored balls domed over the ceiling, swooping down in swirls and shapes to meet the concrete floor, which was covered in artificial snow.

There was a giant Christmas tree in the center of the hangar and a forest full of lighted trees and friendly elves. A cookie-decorating station took up one big corner of the room. Another group of elves painted Christmas shapes on the children's faces. And, of course, Santa was in his castle, posing for pictures and handing out presents.

The festive scene jarred with the frustration swirling inside Cole's head. In the three days since the hearing, a group of lawyers had poured over Samuel's will. This morning, they'd all agreed that Cole was a beneficiary, entitled to half of Samuel's estate.

Cole didn't want an inheritance. When he'd come forward and announced himself, he hadn't the slightest inkling he'd be included in the will. He wasn't here to take anything away from Zachary. Still, he'd use the position if it gave them leverage.

"There she is," said Luca. "Beside the Christmas-tree forest."

Cole spotted her. As always, he was immediately struck by her beauty. She wore a bright red dress with white piping. It clung to her slender curves.

He was here to talk. But talking was far down on his wish list. For starters, he wanted to haul her off somewhere and kiss her senseless.

"Mr. Henderson," Sidney Raines greeted him cheerfully, shaking his hand. "I heard the estate was settled this morning in your favor."

"Call me Cole. It's nice to see you again, Sidney."

Of all the vice presidents, Sidney was easily the more savvy and most reasonable. Cole also liked Max. He was less impressed with Julius, and he was prepared to fight long and hard against Roth.

"It's probably early on to broach the subject," said Sidney, glancing around the huge building, "and I realize this isn't the time or the place, but have you given any thought to what role you'll take on in the company?"

"It isn't the time or the place," said Cole. "But you're right to ask the question. Would you be able to meet over the weekend?"

"Absolutely. You just name the time and place."

Cole took out his cell phone. "If you give me your cell number, I'll call you later on."

Sidney dictated his phone number, then bowed out.

"It's a good question," said Luca.

"I know," said Cole as the two men started toward the brightly lit forest.

"Do you have any idea what you are going to do?"

Cole's thinking hadn't made it past the first couple of moves. "I'm going to find a permanent president."

He worked fourteen-hour days taking care of Aviation 58. He had to get back there as soon as possible. But he'd accepted that he now had a role in protecting Zachary's inheritance.

The closer they got to Amber, the more beautiful she became. No surprise to Cole.

Zachary was in her arms, also dressed in red and white, a goofy little hat on his head. Cole couldn't help but smile at how Zachary reached for the twinkling lights of the closest tree. He'd really missed the little guy.

But then Amber saw him.

Her smile instantly disappeared, and her blue eyes went cold. She took a step, and it was obvious she was going to flee.

Cole quickly crossed the space between them, wrapping a hand around her arm and keeping her close.

Luca wisely hung back.

"Everybody's watching," he cautioned her in a low tone. "Smile. Pretend it's all good between us."

"Go away."

"Not a chance. Smile."

Zachary zeroed in on Cole.

"Gak baw," he called, lurching toward Cole.

Cole reflexively reached for him. His arm brushed her breast, and the contact sent a surge of energy through his body.

He ordered himself to calm the heck down. "You heard the decision on the will?"

Amber put a brittle smile in place, but her tone was flat. "Congratulations."

"We have to talk."

"I don't have time. I promised Zachary we'd decorate some gingerbread." She reached for the baby, but he turned his head, clinging tighter to Cole.

"It'll be easier if I come with you," said Cole.

"No, it won't."

"I'm on your side."

She scoffed out a laugh. "Is that a joke?" Then she held out her arms to Zachary. "Come on, pumpkin."

The baby stayed firmly latched to Cole.

Cole couldn't help feeling sympathetic. "As much as I hate to think about it, I must look like Samuel. Or maybe I sound like him, or smell like him."

"Zachary loves me, too, you know."

"Of course he does."

"He's known me since birth."

"It's a case of mistaken identity," said Cole. "Somewhere in his subconscious, he sees me as family."

"You are family."

Cole was growing more and more conscious of the interest in their conversation. Nobody had dared come within hearing distance, but there was a lot of pointing and whispering going on amongst the staff.

"Let's go decorate some gingerbread."

"Why can't you just leave?"

"If I give him back, he's going to make a scene."

"Was that your plan? I mean today's plan—use Zachary against me?"

"There was no plan."

"Do I strike you as stupid?"

"Amber, please. Gingerbread. Let's just do the gingerbread."

There must have been a note of desperation in his tone that got her attention because she glanced around, seeming to become aware of the onlookers.

"Right," she agreed. "Let's go."

They moved casually to the rear corner of the hangar. People eyed them speculatively as they did so, but held back. Luca disappeared, obviously understanding that Cole needed to speak with Amber alone.

"Mr. Henderson, Ms. Welsley, Merry Christmas!" called a middle-aged woman as they passed.

"Merry Christmas," Cole automatically returned.

"Notice you got top billing," Amber muttered.

"I'm carrying the little rich kid."

"You are the little rich kid."

The greeting seemed to break the ice, and they were bombarded with well-wishers all along their route.

Amber was right. While the employees were completely polite and respectful to her, Cole was getting the lion's share of the attention.

Finally, they came to the cookie-decorating station. The attendants quickly cleared a stand-up table for them, spreading out a new paper cover and bringing an assortment of gingerbread, sugar-cookie shapes, icing and colorful candies.

"Go for it," said Cole. "Pretend you're completely absorbed in the cookies, and maybe people will stay away."

She stared at the tabletop without moving.

"The tree," Cole prompted. "Decorate the tree with the green icing."

Amber picked up a plastic knife.

He focused on keeping his expression agreeable as he spoke. "I'm going to need your support."

She gave another strained smile as she iced the sugar cookie tree. "Like that's going to happen."

"I didn't know about the will."

"Yes, you did."

"How would I know? Tell me how I would know."

"There were ten people in the first reading. Obviously someone leaked the details to you."

"None of them knew I existed."

"So you say."

His voice rose. "I don't just say. It's true."

"The red candies?" she asked him sweetly. "Or the blue and white?"

He took a calming breath. "The red."

"I like the blue and white."

"Seriously? You want to argue about candies?"

"I don't want to argue about anything. I want you to go away. Preferably far away. I hear Alaska's nice this time of year."

Cole shifted Zachary in his arms. Happily, the baby was fascinated by the lights, the sounds and the people moving around.

"If you'll listen to what I have to say, you'll understand why you need to help me."

"No, Cole. If I believed what you had to say, I might be inclined to help you. But that's never going to happen. I'm never going to trust you again."

"I want what's best for Zachary."

"You want what's best for Cole. And congratulations, you're halfway there."

Cole regrouped. "Roth can still take control of the company."

She dropped a handful of blue and white candies on the freshly iced tree and pressed them firmly down with her palm.

For a moment, he thought she'd crush the cookie.

"I can see you've done the math on the share ownership," she said.

"Do you have any influence with the minor shareholders?"

She flashed another phony smile. "None whatsoever. I'm the lowly assistant director of finance and the stepsister of a flaky trophy wife. Why would anyone listen to me?"

"We can still help each other."

"Have a cookie, Cole. It's all you're ever going to get from me."

She suddenly scooped Zachary out of his arms.

It took the baby a second to realize what had happened. Then he immediately opened his mouth and let out a cry.

If not for the staff members surrounding them, Cole would have gone after her. Instead, he watched her march away and disappear into the crowd.

Zachary's cries were soon swallowed by the cheery carols and happy shouts of the other children.

Luca appeared beside him. "Didn't look like that went too well."

"She has *got* to be the most stubborn woman on the planet." Cole's gaze fell to the slightly mangled cookie. He picked it up and took a bite.

"Fighting with Amber makes you hungry?"

"It makes me something, that's for sure."

He crunched down on the sweetness. Fighting made him want to grab her and squeeze her tight, kiss her hard and press their bodies together. It didn't matter what insanity swirled around them, he couldn't forget the night they'd made love, and he couldn't quell the overriding urge to do it all over again.

Amber wasn't going to crack.

It was nearly ten o'clock at night. Zachary had barely napped during the afternoon. He'd fussed through dinner and pouted through his bath. She'd even given him an extra bottle, going through their entire bedtime routine a second time in the hope he'd catch on.

Now he was in his crib, kicking his feet and sobbing. His

covers were on the floor. His head was sweaty, and his hands were wrapped tightly around the painted bars.

Her phone rang over the noise, and for a crazy second she hoped it was Cole. If he called her and asked to come over, it wasn't the same as giving in, was it?

Unfortunately, the number was Destiny's.

She moved into the hallway, and Zachary's cries increased behind her.

"Hi," she said into the phone.

"How're you doing?"

"Not great."

"Is that Zachary?"

Amber leaned against the wall of the hallway, sliding down to sit on the plush carpet. "He doesn't want to settle."

"I'm sorry."

"Not your fault. Not even his fault. Honestly, I feel like sobbing right along with him."

"Luca said you saw Cole today?"

Amber knew she should remember his annoying behavior, her anger and his new set of lies. But instead she remembered his touch, his voice and those now-familiar gray eyes.

"At the kids' party," she answered Destiny. "Wait, when did you see Luca?"

"Earlier tonight."

"Why?" What was going on?

"Nothing's going on. I like Luca, Amber. I'm not giving him any information. He's not even trying to ask. We both know we have to be circumspect."

Amber clunked her head back against the cool wall. "I'm sorry. You're entitled to a personal life."

"He did say something, though."

"What's that?"

"He said that by not helping Cole, you're de facto helping Roth."

Amber gave a slightly hysterical laugh. "I thought you were going to say something much more personal. Like you had beautiful eyes or he wanted to see you naked."

"Oh, he definitely wants to see me naked."

Amber firmly pushed her own problems away. "You should let him."

"Excuse me?"

"You want to. I can hear it in your voice."

"There's nothing in my voice that says—"

"Go for it. Your celibacy won't help me. In fact, it'll probably distract you from helping me."

"You want me to have a one-night stand?"

"I had one." The memories rose one by one in Amber's mind. Into the silence, Destiny's tone turned reflective. "You think you're the better for it?"

"Not at all. But I'm stuck in the middle of a preposterous circumstance. You'll be fine."

"You want some company? Need some reinforcements?"

"You don't need to come all the way over here."

Not that Amber wouldn't welcome the support. Maybe Destiny could take a turn holding Zachary. He was still crying, and it was all but impossible to steel herself against his sadness.

"I'm five minutes away," said Destiny.

"You are?"

"Just left a meeting at Bacharat's. You know, that private lawyers' club? You're on my route home."

"Then, yes, sure. Stop by."

"Sounds good. It might take me a few minutes to park."

"See you then." Amber disconnected the call.

Feeling a bit lighter, she headed back into Zachary's bedroom. He had pulled up on his feet and was gripping the top of the crib rail. His cheeks were flushed red and damp with tears.

"Oh, sweetheart," she said out loud, lifting him into her arms. "How can I help?"

He cried harder.

She racked her brain. "What about some music? Want to watch videos?"

Zachary seemed to have a fondness for country and western, especially the drawling male singers.

With no better ideas, she carried him to the living room and tuned in the country station. It didn't fix the problem, but at least it gave something to blend with his cries.

Then the knock came on her door.

"I know you're too young to understand," she said to Zachary as they crossed the living room, "but my arms are about to get a rest, and that's a very good thing."

She swung open the door.

Cole stood in front of her, Otis at his heels.

She was stunned. "You're supposed to be Destiny."

"I saw her in the lobby."

At the sound of Cole's voice, Zachary swung around.

"She said she'd give me ten minutes," said Cole.

"Destiny sent you up?" Amber didn't want to believe it.

Zachary reached for Cole.

"You want me to take him?"

Amber caved. "She'll be up in ten minutes?"

Cole cracked a smile. "I bet he's asleep by then. He looks exhausted."

Amber was weak. In fact, she was defeated. "He's the one and only reason I'll let you in."

"I'll take it." Cole gathered Zachary against his shoulder and moved into the foyer.

"What's goin' on here, partner?" Cole rumbled.

Zachary laid his head onto Cole's shoulder and his cries turned to shuddering breaths.

She couldn't resist. She smoothed the sweat from Zachary's forehead, brushing her fingers across his downy, fine hair. "Poor little guy."

"You're very patient," said Cole.

"Not always."

There were times when she couldn't help feeling frustrated and resentful. She was doing everything she could for Zachary, but it wasn't enough. Sometimes she thought he was being miserable just to make her jump through hoops. But in her saner moments, she knew he was far too young to be manipulative.

"You need to do anything?" he asked her as they walked to the living room. "Hungry, thirsty?"

"Don't be nice."

A smirk appeared on his face. "Okay."

"You know what I mean. Don't try to ingratiate yourself by helping me with Zachary. It won't work."

Otis picked a spot beside an armchair and flopped down.

"Then do you think you could whip something up for me?" asked Cole. "Maybe a dry martini and a few hors d'oeuvres?"

"Shut up and mind the baby."

Cole grinned. "He's doing fine."

"I hate that you can do that, you know." It wasn't fair at all.

"Accident of genetics." Cole lowered himself into an armchair.

It was yet another thing that ticked her off. When she was soothing Zachary, she couldn't sit down. She had to stand and sway or he'd cry his head off.

"This whole thing is an accident of genetics," Cole repeated.

"You want some hot cocoa?" she asked. She couldn't help remembering the last time they'd shared that particular beverage, but she needed something soothing right now.

"I was just messing with you. Don't go to any trouble."

But it wasn't any trouble. "It'll only take a minute, and I'm having some."

He hesitated. "In that case, sure."

She left for the kitchen.

"You need any help?" he called behind her.

"You're already helping."

"Points for that?" he asked.

The question stopped her cold. She couldn't help remembering the last time they'd joked about points. He'd asked to spend the night, then they'd slept curled together in her bed. If only they could go back to that moment, even just for a little while. Because what she really needed right now was a broad shoulder to lean on. Unfortunately, leaning on Cole's shoulder was out of the question.

She heated up the cocoa and returned to the living room.

"Sorry," he told her.

"For what?" She set a steaming cup down on the small table beside him and took the end of the sofa opposite to where he sat.

"For making that points crack."

He obviously remembered the last time.

The sweetened air seemed to still around them. Her mouth went dry, and her heartbeat thudded thickly in her chest. She braved a look at his face, and their gazes held. The ticking of the clock seemed to grow louder.

Cole broke the silence. "The reason I'm here…"

She was half afraid, half excited about what he might say. She distracted herself with a sip.

"The reason I'm here," he began again, "is because we can't let Roth win, and that means I need your help."

She didn't want Roth to win. But she didn't want Cole to win, either. Her throat closed up, and her chest pierced with pain.

She had a desperate urge to rip Zachary from his arms. She didn't care if he cried. She didn't care if she never slept again. She wanted to hold him every second of every day from now until someone forced her to stop.

"I…" she tried. "How can…" To her mortification, a tear slipped out.

She rose from her chair, surreptitiously swiping the tear away. "He's asleep. We can put him in his crib now."

"Sure," Cole agreed easily, rising with Zachary in his arms, watching her closely.

She walked down the hall to the nursery. There, she straightened the rumpled sheets and folded a fresh blanket onto the mattress.

A yellow nightlight glowed in the corner, highlighting the cartoon giraffes, elephants and lions on the wall. Soft stuffed animals decorated every surface.

Cole moved beside her and eased Zachary down onto the white flannel sheet. He pulled his arm from beneath Zachary and stepped back. The baby didn't stir. Amber covered Zachary with a knit blanket and a patchwork quilt. Then she stroked her palm over his warm forehead.

"Good night, sweetheart," she whispered.

She straightened, her heart aching all over again. She gripped the top of the crib rail, struggling to draw a breath.

Cole's strong hand came down on her shoulder. "Are you okay?" he asked softly.

She swallowed. Her voice came out on a pained whisper. "I'm so frightened."

"I know."

She shook her head. "No, you don't. You can't possibly understand."

She was going to lose Zachary, and there wasn't a thing she could do about it.

He gently turned her. She didn't stop him as he drew her into his arms. It didn't seem to matter that he was one of the enemies; she accepted the strength he offered.

His voice was deep and steady. "I know you can't let yourself believe anything I say. But I want what's best for Zachary. I promise I'll do what's best for Zachary."

She tipped her chin to gaze up at him. She wanted so badly to believe it was true. She needed some hope to hang on to.

Minutes ticked slowly past.

He reached up to brush her chin, his voice low and sexy. "You are amazing."

She knew she had to pull away. She had to shut this down before it went any further. His eyes were smoldering, his desire completely obvious. His hand crept into her hair. His gaze zeroed in on her lips, and he bent his head.

He was going to kiss her.

She wasn't going to stop him.

His lips touched hers, warm, soft and gentle.

She stretched up, leaned in, let her arms twine around his neck as he took the kiss deeper. She'd missed him. She couldn't believe how much she'd missed him.

Her world was dissolving around her, and he felt like the only anchor point. His hand splayed her back, pressing her close. A moan rose up from her chest, and she met his tongue. Flicking flames of desire rose up inside her, heating her body, sensitizing every nerve ending. She needed to get closer, to feel his skin.

But suddenly, he drew back. "We can't do this."

She was mortified. What was she thinking? What was she doing, throwing herself into his arms?

He braced his hands around her upper arms, putting a few inches between them. "We need to talk."

"Talk," Amber managed to agree.

He put a hand lightly on the small of her back, guiding her from the nursery, down the hall, back to the living room.

She went straight to the far corner of the sofa, struggling to pull her dignity around her.

She could feel Cole's gaze on her from where he sat in the armchair. But she couldn't bring herself to look at him. She couldn't imagine what he thought of her. He'd deceived her, used her to gain information about Coast Eagle, Samuel and Zachary. And yet she'd been willing to leap into bed with him a second time.

There was something terribly wrong with her.

"What will Roth do?" Cole asked into the silence. "If he wins custody, what will he do?"

Amber struggled to move past emotion to logic. "I expect he will hire a nanny. I hope he keeps Isabel, but I don't know that he will." She had to stop for a breath. "Then he'll use the power of his guardianship to get appointed president of Coast Eagle."

"He won't want to be chairman of the board?"

"He wants to be hands-on. He wants to run the company day-to-day. His first plan is to update or replace the entire fleet. He thinks he'll be able to increase our market share enough to cover the debt."

"You doubt that?" asked Cole.

"His projections are dangerously optimistic."

Cole gave a contemplative nod.

Amber forced herself to ask the burning question. "What will you do?"

His gaze was level and honest. "I don't know."

"How can I trust you?"

"You can't. You shouldn't."

She scoffed out a laugh at that.

He took a sip of his now-cool cocoa. "All you can do right now is go on what's certain. Roth's got the advantage over me, and he cares about Roth, first, last and always."

"You're saying you're the lesser of two evils."

"I know you can't bring yourself to trust me yet. But you know for certain you can't trust Roth."

"That's not at all comforting."

"I know. But it's all you've got."

Amber knew he was right. She hated it. But it was true.

Nine

As a significant shareholder in Coast Eagle, no matter how things turned out in the long term, Cole knew he needed to understand the company. He and Luca had both been in daily contact with Aviation 58 since arriving in Atlanta, but Luca now offered to take over as much as possible on the Alaska operation.

Luckily, even leading into the busy holiday travel season, things seemed well under control at Aviation 58. There were no unexpected maintenance issues, passenger load was as predicted and the Alaskan weather was cooperating surprisingly well.

Cole entered the Coast Eagle building and was immediately recognized. Security greeted him and called up to the executive floor to announce his arrival.

As he exited the elevator, he was greeted by the receptionist, Sandra, who was exceedingly welcoming and polite this time. She introduced him to Samuel's personal assistant, a fiftyish man named Bartholomew Green. Bartholomew had a British accent and was dressed in a dark formal suit, a matching vest, crisp white shirt and a gold tie.

Samuel's office was also ostentatious, with a huge, ornately carved cherrywood desk, and a massive credenza with cut-glass decanters. A sofa and two armchairs had diamond tufted, dark leather upholstery, while expensive oil paintings hung on the walls. Cole couldn't help wonder how his down-to-earth mother had fallen in love with the man he was learning about.

"Will you be moving into the office today, sir?" asked Bartholomew.

"I will," said Cole.

The last thing in the world he wanted to do was step into his father's shoes. But he needed to make a statement. Roth, the judge and everybody else had to see he was taking the reins—even if it was only temporary.

He took in Bartholomew's attire once more. He supposed

he'd have to update his own wardrobe, and he was going to make the same recommendation to Amber. She was next on his list of things to deal with at Coast Eagle.

"Can you set up a meeting with Max and the vice presidents for this afternoon?" Cole asked Bartholomew.

"Do you have a preferred time, sir?"

"Two o'clock." Cole couldn't have cared less about the time, but he needed to be the guy making the decisions.

"The east boardroom?"

"Sounds fine. Can you direct me to Amber Welsley's office?"

"She's in accounting. That's on the seventh floor. Shall I show you the way?"

"Is it overly complicated?"

Bartholomew seemed to allow himself a small smile. "Left when you get off the elevator, first hallway on your right."

"I think I can manage. No need for a tour guide."

"Very good, sir."

"Anything else I should know?" Cole asked, curious to know where Bartholomew's loyalties would lie.

"What would you like to know?"

Cole paused to gauge the man's expression. "What do you think is important?"

An intelligent light came into Bartholomew's eyes. "Mr. Henderson had a lot of faith in Sidney. I believe that was appropriate. He also had a lot of faith in Roth. I believe that faith may have been misplaced. He also understood the need to deploy Julius in certain situations."

"Such as?"

"Would you like me to be blunt?"

"Always."

"Julius is a pit bull. But he's Coast Eagle's pit bull."

"What about Max Cutter?"

"Max Cutter will be completely up front and honest with you. If I had to guess, I'd say he can't wait to get out of the president's role and back to the legal department."

Cole agreed with that assessment. Max had said as much himself.

"And Amber Welsley?" Cole asked.

"I knew Mrs. Henderson a lot better than I knew Ms. Welsley."

"Impressions?"

"She has always struck me as hardworking but below the radar. I'm not certain she thought very highly of Mr. Samuel Henderson."

"He married her baby sister."

"Indeed. Though I'm not certain she was a fan of Mrs. Henderson, either."

"May I rely on your discretion, Bartholomew?"

"You may."

"Good to know." Cole was impressed with the man so far.

"If I may, sir?"

"Yes?"

"You haven't asked about Samuel Henderson."

"That's because I don't want to know."

Bartholomew was silent for a moment. "Very good."

"Is that a problem for you?"

"Not at all."

Cole looked through the doorway to the outer office and Bartholomew's desk. "Give me the lay of the land here."

Bartholomew moved to stand beside him. "You've seen reception, and my desk is right there. The office to your right is the president's. Max isn't using it, because he already has an office on this floor. Around the corner to your left is Roth, next to him is Julius, and Sidney is around the corner from the president's office. The east boardroom is next to Sidney, and the west meeting room is next to Julius. After that, you're through reception to the director's offices and the executive lunch room."

"Is everyone in today?"

"As I understand it, yes."

"Thank you, Bartholomew." Cole exited the office and made his way to the elevator in the reception area.

Under Sandra's veiled curiosity, he pressed the button for seven. He could well imagine the conversations and speculation would start the second the door closed behind him. That was good. He wanted people to wonder.

On the seventh floor, he took a left then a right, quickly finding Amber's office.

Her door was open, and he was taken aback by the small size. She sat at her desk, head down, writing on a financial sheet.

"There's an adding error on report sixteen," she said without looking up, obviously hearing him arrive. "I know we have to pull the soft commitments in manually, but we need to make sure the formulas are—"

She spotted Cole in the doorway. "Sorry." His presence seemed to fluster her. "I assumed you were my assistant."

"Nope." He walked in.

She sat up straight and set down her pen. "You're here."

"I'm here." He glanced around. "More to the point, you're *here*."

"I'm usually here."

"This is your office?"

"It is."

"So the office of the assistant director of finance?"

"That would be me."

He braced himself on the desk across from her. "Not anymore."

She drew back. "Have I been fired?"

"Promoted. Or haven't you been paying attention?"

"Being temporarily nominated as guardian is not a promotion."

"You're chair of the board."

"For the next five minutes."

"If you want people to take you seriously, you need to look the part."

"Pretending I'm the real chair of the board would be embarrassing for everyone involved."

He straightened. "I don't get you."

"I'm not that complicated."

"Yes, you are. But that's not my point. We need to use every weapon at our disposal. One of the strongest, if not *the* strongest we have is the fact that, for now, we *are* in charge. Get up."

Her brows shot up. "Excuse me?"

"There's an empty office on the top floor—you're moving in. Right now."

"You can't order me to—"

"Amber."

She set her jaw.

He ignored the expression. "Your biggest weakness is that nobody can picture you at the helm."

"That's because I'm not capable of taking the helm."

"Who says?"

"Reason and good judgment?"

"They're wrong. And you're wrong." His tone hardened. This was too important to mess up. "And if you don't march yourself up to that corner office right now and start giving orders, then you haven't done your best by Zachary."

"I have done everything—"

"No, Amber. You haven't. Right now, between the two of us, we control sixty-five percent of Coast Eagle. Let's start acting like it. Let's let the world see us at the helm. That way, they'll know we can do it."

She glanced around her office, the three computer screens, the stacks of reports. "But—"

"First stop, your boss's office to give him permission to replace you."

"Give away my job?" The prospect clearly distressed her.

"Temporarily. Trust me, Amber. And if you can't trust me, trust Destiny. Phone her now. I know she'll agree."

Amber's lips compressed as she obviously thought through the situation.

"Being seen in charge is our best weapon," he reiterated. "Don't throw it away."

"Okay." She came to her feet, expression determined. "I'm willing to try anything."

Cole felt a surge of relief. He'd known she was stubborn. But he'd also known she was smart. Luckily, smart had won out.

* * *

"I've never even set foot in this store," Amber whispered to Destiny.

The next step in Cole's stated strategy was to deck both of them out in what he called a power wardrobe. From what Amber could see, that meant spending a whole lot of money.

"I've never shopped here, either," Destiny answered. "But I know some of the senior partners do. I've heard them mention the name."

"I don't dare look at the price tags," said Amber, glancing around at the gleaming floors, marble pillars and leather furniture groupings with complimentary designer water and champagne.

"What price tags?" asked Destiny. "If you have to ask, you can't afford it."

"I think I might break out in hives."

Cole and Luca entered the store behind them.

"This ought to do it," said Luca with obvious satisfaction.

Cole took in the high, brightly lit ceilings. "It's nothing like the Fashion Farm back home."

"Are you two going upstairs?" Destiny nodded to the sign for menswear.

"And miss the fun?" asked Luca.

"Let's get Amber decked out first," said Cole. "I want to make sure she doesn't hold back."

"You doubt my powers of persuasion?" asked Destiny.

"You'll make me self-conscious," Amber told Cole.

"What better means to cure you? If you can get comfortable in front of me, the rest of the executives will be easy." He pointed to a headless mannequin in a blazer and skirt combination. "What about that?"

The skirt was short and black, scattered with tiny white flecks. The blouse was white with a braided scooped neck. And the blazer was solid black, fitted, with the sleeves pushed up the forearms.

"I like the necklace, too," said Cole. "And the belt. Why not try on the whole thing?"

"You don't think the skirt's a little short?" Amber asked. Though she would admit, the outfit looked fun.

"Shows you have confidence," said Cole.

"I don't have confidence."

Cole turned to Destiny. "You see what I'm dealing with?"

"It would work with black stockings," said Destiny.

Cole opened his mouth, but Luca elbowed him in the ribs.

A sales clerk arrived. "Do you need any help?" she asked with a broad smile.

Amber couldn't help wondering what Cole had been about to say on the topic of black stockings. She also couldn't seem to stop a shimmer of sexual awareness.

"She needs a whole new wardrobe," said Cole, gesturing to Amber.

Amber shifted under everyone's scrutiny. "Oh, I wouldn't say I need an entire—"

"Shut up," Destiny interrupted. She gestured back to Cole. "He's buying, and we need her to look like a million bucks. Literally."

"Daywear, evening, office?" the clerk asked.

"Yes," said Cole.

"This is getting out of hand," said Amber.

She understood the principle behind his strategy. And now that she'd had a few hours to think about it, she agreed with it. But still, it wasn't necessary to go overboard.

"She's been appointed to chair the board of a billion-dollar company," said Cole.

Amber opened her mouth to disagree, but his look stopped her. Fine. Okay. She was going to stop telling people she was a fraud. She was still a fraud, but she could fake it for Zachary's sake.

"Bring it on," she said to the clerk. "I need to look good in the office. I have several evening meetings scheduled, and given the season, there are a few formal events, as well."

"She'll need shoes and purses," said Destiny.

"Don't forget jewelry," said Luca.

"Do we want to do something with her hair?" asked Cole.

Amber glared at him. "Careful. You're next."

"I'm perfectly willing to get a haircut."

"He's the…" Amber paused. "What is your title? You're going to need a title. I'm thinking a big, brass plate on the office door, Mr. Henderson."

"The Big Cheese?" joked Luca.

Destiny gave him a thumbs-down.

The clerk smirked as she began looking through the well-spaced racks.

"Grand Pooh-Bah," said Cole.

"I'm not joking," said Amber. "This is your plan. You need to buy all the way in."

"We've got a president. We've got a chair. Executive board member?"

"You can be the chair," said Amber. "I'll be an executive board member."

"Cochair," said Luca. He pointed to Amber. "Cochair of the board." Then he pointed to Cole. "Cochair of the board."

Amber and Cole looked at each other.

"Okay by me," she said. It would be better than doing it alone.

Cole shrugged. "I'll order the brass nameplates."

"What do you think of these?" asked the clerk, holding a gold dress and a black blazer in one hand, and a navy-and-white outfit with a nautical flair in the other.

"The stuff on the mannequin, too," said Cole.

Amber gave in. "Sure. Bring me whatever you think will work. I'm new at this."

The clerk showed her to an airy changing room with a settee and a triple mirror.

"Come out and show us," Cole called.

"I'm going in to help," said Destiny, slipping past the velvet curtain.

The professional outfits were easy to find. But once they switched to dresses, things bogged down. There were simply too many choices, and all of them were gorgeous. Once she made it past her cost worries, Amber actually began to enjoy herself.

After an hour, Cole headed to menswear. Once he was gone,

Destiny dived into the fun, trying on a few of the dresses herself. The women were close enough in size that they could swap back and forth. Destiny was a little bigger in the bust while Amber had the longer legs. Some of the swaps were quite comical.

Amber had accepted a glass of champagne, and now wandered over to where it sat on a glass table. She was trying on a flirty, strapless cocktail dress that was unlike anything she'd ever worn before.

The bodice was snug, wrapping her in silver beading and sequins. It had a high waist of deep jewel blue with a chiffon skirt that flowed to midthigh. Her back was mostly bare, crisscrossed in shiny, beaded straps, ending in a drop V waist. She'd also found a pair of high-heeled silver shoes that were surprisingly comfortable and seemed to go with a lot of outfits.

"*This* is a keeper," said Destiny from behind her.

Amber turned to see Destiny do a runway turn in a glimmering, full-length gold sheath with a slit up the leg.

Luca's voice drawled from the armchair where he'd stayed back to watch. "Have you got a month's pay to blow?"

"I was going to let Cole buy it," Destiny answered with an impish grin. "The man just inherited half a billion dollars. He's not going to notice one little dress."

"Sure," came Cole's unexpected voice. "Dresses are on me."

Amber turned to find him looking her up and down. "Buy that one."

She felt suddenly self-conscious, particularly knowing he'd had a good view of the back.

"I'm just messing around," she told him. "I've already picked out more than enough."

"Buy it," he repeated. "It looks good on you."

"I don't have anywhere to wear it."

"You will."

"I don't think you have a good feel for my social life."

"The Coast Eagle Christmas party is on Friday. It's formal." She glanced down at herself. "You call this formal?"

"What do you call it?"

"Nightclubbing."

"Nobody's going to complain." He moved in a bit closer, his voice going low as Destiny and Cole engaged in their own conversation. "I'm sure not going to complain."

The familiar shiver of arousal teased her limbs. "Stop."

"You done?" he asked.

She nodded.

"Got shoes, purses, jewelry? Whatever else Destiny says you need?"

"I wouldn't trust Destiny if I was you."

"She's right. I did just inherit a ridiculous amount of money. And this is important." There was something in his tone, some combination of reluctance and tenacity.

"Are you okay?" she asked.

"I'm fine."

"Are you still wrapping your head around it?"

It took him a moment to speak. "I don't think I've started wrapping my head around it. I'm going one step at a time. You hungry?"

The question took her by surprise. "Hungry?"

"For tonight, I think that's the next step."

"I could go for a pizza," she admitted. It would feel nice to climb back into her jeans and be normal.

A grin spread across his face. "I like you, Amber. All this, and now you want to go out for pizza."

"Double cheese if you don't mind. And maybe a beer?"

Cole tipped his head to the sales clerk. "We'll take everything she liked, including the dress she's wearing." Then he nodded to Destiny. "Her, too. She's got an important court case coming up, and she needs to look good."

The clerk's eyes went round.

"Cole," Amber protested, horrified to think that the woman might take him seriously and ring up everything.

He ignored her protest, instead speaking to Luca and Destiny. "We're going for pizza and a strategy session. Now that we look the part, we have to act the part. Amber and I need to make a decision. Something important, positive and significant, and we have to be able to implement it fast."

"You mean change company policy?" asked Amber.

"Absolutely," said Cole. "You two get changed, I'll pay the bill."

Amber renewed her protest. "Cole, you can't buy everything."

He slipped an arm around her shoulder. "I know this is hard for you. But we're doing it. And honestly, I'm through having this argument with you."

A spurt of anger jumped to life inside her. She opened her mouth to retort, but something in his eyes stopped her cold.

Fine. He wanted to blow his money? That was up to him. She was through trying to save him from himself.

In her new clothes, and at the head of the boardroom table, Amber looked fantastic. Cole had to struggle to keep from chuckling at how the vice presidents kept shooting surreptitious looks her way. She was wearing a steel-gray blazer and skirt set, with a white blouse underneath. Lace along the scooped neckline kept the outfit from being too severe.

She'd changed her hairstyle, too. Strands were braided at her temples and partially pulled back to a knot at the nap of her neck. She looked sophisticated and professional. She also looked sexy, and it made him want to kiss her.

Then again, pretty much everything made him want to kiss her these days. Last night, watching her bite into a slice of double-cheese pizza had turned him on.

He dragged his gaze away from her, focusing on business. He and Amber both looked the part now, and they were going to act it, too, starting with some small but definitive strategic directions for the company.

"Thank you all for joining us," Cole opened politely, although everyone in the room was fully aware their attendance at the senior management meeting had not been optional.

"Ms. Welsley and I realize this is a temporary situation," he continued. "However, our expectation is that the status quo will continue into the future."

"Excuse me?" Roth piped up.

Cole sent him a glare and kept speaking. "My interest in Coast Eagle is not in dispute, and I'll be relying on Ms. Welsley for continuity."

Roth opened his mouth, but Cole spoke right over him. "For the moment, Ms. Welsley has made a few decisions about passenger compensation."

"Thank you, Cole," said Amber, her tone crisp, her posture straight. "As most of you know, new guidelines on passenger compensation were developed by the U.S. Consumer Association in October of this year."

"Voluntary guidelines," said Roth.

"Roth," said Cole. "If you could please hold your comments."

Roth's eyes blazed at the rebuke while Max obviously fought a smirk. Sidney also looked like he was enjoying himself.

"Accounting has done a comparison between overbooked flights, passenger compensation and lost passenger revenue due to last minute cancellations. Bartholomew, can you put up the slides?"

Bartholomew, who also looked a bit smug, brought up the graphic slides on the side screen.

"As you can see," said Amber, "with a change in our policy on flight overbooking, actual monetary loss will be manageable, while the marketing and social media attention, not to mention the customer confidence and goodwill could be significant. Therefore, we'll immediately adopt the new guidelines on passenger compensation and suspend the policy that allows overbooking. That way, our customers can be completely confident in their travel plans."

She stopped speaking and looked levelly down the table.

Cole felt an immediate surge of pride. She was damn good at this.

"May we speak now?" asked Roth, sarcasm dripping from his tone.

"Yes," Amber answered, even though the question was directed at Cole.

Cole's pride in her increased.

"The monetary losses will be significant," said Roth.

"Loses will be compensated for in the long run," said Amber.

"Maybe in a best-case scenario. But passengers don't want certainty. They want low prices. If you drive our prices up by even ten dollars a ticket, they leave for the competition in droves."

"I'm not suggesting we change our prices," said Amber.

"You're living in fantasyland," Roth all but shouted. "Do you have any idea what kind of a mess you'll leave for me to clean up?"

Though he was trying to let Amber take the lead, Cole couldn't help himself. "You?"

Roth seemed to catch himself. "Us."

"Well, *us,*" said Cole, "is Ms. Welsley and me. And I agree with her assessment."

"I agree with it, too," said Max. He looked to Sidney. "Can you work up a marketing plan? We'll need to hit the ground running as soon as the announcement is made."

"I want to announce right away," said Amber with both clarity and confidence. "I want passengers to know their remaining holiday travel plans will not be disrupted by overbooking."

"The Friends and Family campaign is nearly finished," said Sidney. "We can easily incorporate this as a marquee element."

"Done," said Max.

"Hold on," said Roth. "We haven't heard from Julius."

Julius's chin came up. He looked a bit like a deer in the headlights. It was clear he didn't know where to jump.

"Julius reports to Max," said Cole. "Max has made his decision."

"That's not how it works," Roth shouted.

"That's how it works now," said Cole. "This meeting is adjourned." He turned his attention to the president, clearly dismissing everyone else. "Max, do you have a second?"

"I do," said Max.

Fury in his eyes, Roth rocked back from the table and stomped from the room.

With an admirably contained smirk, Bartholomew closed the door behind them all, leaving Cole, Amber and Max alone.

"At the risk of speaking out of turn," said Max, "that was fun."

Amber blew out a breath and slouched down in her chair. "That's not the word I would use."

Cole gave in to the urge to place a hand on her shoulder. "You did great."

"He is out for blood."

"He was always out for blood," said Max.

"You don't think he'd ever take it out on Zachary, do you?"

The slight tremor in her voice told Cole just how brilliantly she'd been acting while the vice presidents were in the room.

"He won't have the chance. Because we're going to win." Cole refused to contemplate anything else.

He turned his attention to Max. "They're resuming the custody hearing on the twenty-eighth."

"Next week?"

Cole nodded.

"Who's representing you?"

"Since Amber is supporting my petition for custody, Destiny has agreed to represent me. She knows the background and circumstances better than anyone else I could hire."

Max's brow furrowed. "She's not the most experienced choice."

"Her firm has assigned a senior partner for support. And they've earmarked their top research team. I'm guessing they want my future business."

"Then that's the best of both worlds," said Max, his expression relaxing.

"That's what we thought." Cole covered Amber's hand with his.

Hers was cold.

Max spoke up. "You know Roth's out there soliciting the support of the minor shareholders."

"He's got the advantage in that," said Amber, sliding her hand from beneath Cole's.

"He does," Max agreed. "They all know him. And Samuel's vote of confidence goes a long way. And, I'm sorry to be so blunt, Amber, but they all knew Coco. That doesn't work in our favor."

"We've got genetics on our side," said Cole.

Cole felt no admiration whatsoever for his father. But he'd quickly come to care about his half brother. And he cared more about Amber than he could have imagined. She was desperately trying to do the right thing, and the jackals were circling her now.

"Can you see any problem with the policy change?" he asked Max.

"None," said Max.

"Any questions?" asked Cole.

"Not yet." Max paused. "Anything else you need right now?"

Cole looked to Amber, and she shook her head.

"We're good," said Cole.

Max rose to leave, closing the door behind him and leaving them alone.

"You did it," said Cole.

"I sure hope it works."

"It will. And so will the others. This one was a good idea, a solid business decision. As the first airline to adopt the guidelines, you're going to get some really positive buzz. The policy change will garner loyalty—maybe not all of your passengers, but enough. And those passengers will be the frequent fliers. That's huge. It was a smart move you made."

"We made."

"It was a smart move, Amber. Don't sell yourself short. They know who's in charge now, and it'll spread around the building like wildfire."

"You think?" She seemed to ponder. "Sidney might tell someone. But Roth will never admit it. And Bartholomew doesn't strike me as a gossip."

"I'm willing to bet Bartholomew knows exactly when and how much to gossip."

"Phase three underway?" she asked.

"Phase three well underway." He jokingly held out his hand. She accepted it and shook.

The contact made him instantly recall what it was like to hold her close. He wished he could pull her in for a hug. He longed to kiss her. He longed to stroke her hair and feel the length of her body pressed up against his.

"Destiny will be here in an hour," she said, retrieving her hand once again.

Cole accepted her withdrawal, shaking off his wayward feelings. "Destiny's been looking up precedents for blood relatives being given preference in custody cases. Do you know if Roth spent any amount of time with Zachary?"

"Not that I heard about, but Coco didn't tell me everything."

"I've been trying to predict his thinking," said Cole. "With you, his best ammunition was that you were too inexperienced to run Coast Eagle. With me, he'll go after my capability as Zachary's guardian. I'm vulnerable there."

"Not if they ask Zachary."

Cole chuckled at that. "It is too bad that Zachary can't talk."

"It's too bad Zachary's not a puppy."

"Excuse me?"

"With a puppy, you put him down between the two people and both call him. Whoever the dog runs to wins."

Cole grinned. "I do like my chances with that."

"Sometimes the simplest solutions work best."

"Can we suggest it to the judge?"

"Only if you want him to order a psychological evaluation."

Ten

Christmas Eve, Amber and Destiny had settled down in a corner of the penthouse living room in front of the twinkling tree and the gas fireplace, cups of eggnog in their hands. Zachary was bathed and wearing red-and-white snowflake pajamas. They'd already snapped a few pictures of him looking so adorable, and now he was busy pulling himself up on pieces of furniture, trying to toddle from one handhold to the next, falling down on his diapered bottom with each attempt.

"At least he's tenacious," said Destiny.

"Stubborn," said Amber. "And not always in a good way."

But she had to admire him in this. He picked himself up again, gripped the coffee table, made it to standing, then set his sights on the ottoman.

"Is it just me," asked Amber, "or does he seem extraordinarily intelligent?"

"He seems extraordinarily intelligent."

"I thought so. I only had to tell him once to leave the tree alone."

"And here I thought the pine needles prickled his hands."

"Maybe," Amber allowed. "Do you mind very much that we're staying in tonight?"

Over the past few years, she and Destiny had always travelled somewhere fun for Christmas. Last December they'd gone snowboarding at a great resort in Switzerland. This year, travelling would have been a lot more complicated with Zachary along. Amber knew it would be better relaxing at home. She also wanted to keep him in his routine, since tomorrow would be such an exciting day.

She knew he had no concept of Santa and wouldn't even realize the presents had appeared overnight. Still, she found herself looking forward to the morning. She was certain he'd take to unwrapping just fine. And she hoped he'd like playing with the toys she'd picked out.

"Not at all. This is fun, too," said Destiny. "The eggnog's fantastic. And the view from here is great."

"What about Luca?" Amber asked. She'd been curious about their budding relationship for days now. But whenever she and Destiny were together, the court case had taken all of their attention.

"He's still in town," said Destiny.

"I *know* he's still in town. I see Cole every day at the office. What I'm asking is if anything has happened between you two?"

"Define *happened*."

"Have you kissed him?"

"A few times." Destiny covered a smile with a sip of eggnog.

"And?"

"And what?"

"And anything more than kissing?"

"Not yet."

"But soon?"

"I don't know. Something's holding me back. I guess I'm not the flinging kind. Who knew?"

"Turned out I was," said Amber. "Who knew?"

Destiny's attention perked up. "Again?"

"No, not *again*. The once. I haven't slept with him since I found out the truth."

"But you want to."

"Who wouldn't? But he deceived me, and he's trying to take Zachary away."

"He's trying to keep Zachary away from Roth. That's not quite the same thing."

"It's not," Amber agreed. "I suppose I should be grateful."

"Are you grateful?"

"He's a fascinating guy, Dest. He's incredibly strategic, and unbelievably bold. In less than a week, he's got the entire company in awe of him."

"Controlling the company will do that to people."

"Yeah, but it's more than just that. He's got a certain presence. You should have seen him shut Roth down." Amber remembered the expression on Roth's face. "If Roth ever gets a chance, he's going to annihilate Cole."

"I don't think he'll get the chance," said Destiny.

Amber looked closely at her expression. "Are you really that optimistic? Or are you trying to make me feel good on Christmas Eve."

"Both. But I am optimistic. There are a lot of precedents out there for blood relatives winning custody."

Amber's gaze caught on Zachary. "Look!"

Zachary took a step, then another and another. He sort of toppled into the ottoman, but stayed upright. Then he turned to Amber with a massive, self-satisfied grin on his face.

"Good boy," said Amber, beaming with pride.

"There'll be no stopping him now," said Destiny.

A knock sounded on the door.

Destiny rose. "I'll get it. You keep watch in case he does something else amazing."

Zachary slapped his hands against the leather ottoman. Amber guessed he was gearing up for the next excursion.

Then, suddenly, his face broke into another grin. "Gak baw!" He let go of the ottoman and toddled forward.

"Hey there, partner."

Amber twisted to see Cole entering the room, a couple of brightly wrapped packages tucked under his arm.

Zachary made it three steps, then four, then his pace sped up. A split second later, things got entirely out of control.

Cole shot forward to grab him before he could go head over heels. Otis stayed a safe pace behind.

"Nice job," Cole praised Zachary.

"He just started doing that," said Amber. She found herself ridiculously happy to have Cole share the moment.

"Merry Christmas," came Luca's cheerful voice.

He and Destiny emerged from the foyer, Luca's arm firmly planted around her waist, a sappy grin on his face. Her cheeks were slightly flushed, and her lips were slightly swollen. No need to guess who'd come up with the idea of dropping by tonight.

"I brought you a present," Cole said to Amber.

Her glance went to the packages, instantly guilty because she hadn't bought anything for him. "Oh, Cole, you shouldn't have."

"Oh. Uh…no." He looked contrite. "These are for Zachary."

In his arms, Zachary was already plucking at the ribbons.

"I'm your present."

"Excuse me?" She couldn't believe she'd heard him right, or that he'd made such an outrageous statement in front of Destiny and Luca.

"I'm here to make sure Zachary gets to sleep tonight."

She felt relieved. Or maybe it was disappointed. Sure, it would be mortifying to have Cole show up and announce he wanted to sleep with her. Then again, it would be awfully exciting to have Cole show up and announce he wanted to sleep with her.

She realized everyone was staring at her.

She quickly reined in her wayward thoughts. "You didn't have to do that."

"No trouble. Can I put these under the tree?"

"Sure. Of course. But I can't guarantee Zachary will stay away from them."

Cole looked at the clock. It was coming up on eight.

"He can sit with me for a while," he said. "That should keep him out of trouble."

Otis selected a spot near the tree in front of an armchair and curled up to watch.

"Mind if I steal Destiny?" Luca asked. "We've got a car and a driver, and I want to take in the lights."

"Ask Destiny," said Amber.

"Do you mind?" Destiny asked her.

"Go, go. Have fun. I've got the baby whisperer here to make my life easy."

Luca tugged Destiny against his side. "Your chariot awaits."

Cole set the gifts under the tree while Destiny and Luca all but scampered out the front door.

"Did he drag you here?" asked Amber.

Cole rose, Zachary happily bopping him on the top of the head. "What? Who?"

"Luca. He was pretty single-minded about getting Destiny out the door. I'm assuming you're the sacrificial lamb."

Cole smiled as he lowered himself into an armchair. "I volunteered for the gig."

"You're a good friend."

"I am," he agreed. "Got any more eggnog?"

"I do."

"I can get it myself."

She scooped up Destiny's empty cup. "Oh, no, you don't. You're on baby duty. Just sit tight."

He lifted Zachary into a standing position on his lap. "Oh, I like this," he said to the baby. "You and I hang out here. Your auntie does all the work."

She poured a fresh glass of eggnog and added some spiced rum, stirring the concoction together.

When she returned to the living room, Zachary was sitting facing Cole, playing with the buttons on his denim shirt.

She handed Cole the glass. "Don't let him taste it."

Cole's eyes squinted down. "I wouldn't do that. I won't give him anything without asking you."

"There's rum in it. That's all I meant." She hadn't meant to sound picky and possessive.

Cole took a drink. "Good." Then he set the glass out of reach of Zachary.

The awkward moment passed.

"Nice pajamas this guy's got going on," Cole said easily.

"I couldn't resist them. They were so cute."

"Did you take some pictures?"

"I did."

"Will you take one of the two of us?"

The request surprised her, but she quickly recovered. "Sure." Her phone was on a side table, and she reached to retrieve it.

"How about in front of the tree?" Cole asked Zachary, sitting down on the floor. "Any chance you'll hold still and pose for the camera?"

"Gak baw."

"As always, I'm going to take that as a yes."

Amber lined up the camera, taking various poses from various angles. While she snapped the pictures, the family resemblance between the two became startlingly evident. She was half amazed, half afraid.

It was obvious they belonged together. It was just as obvious that she'd have little say in the matter. And a win for Cole still left her up in the air. Or maybe it was out in the cold.

"Did you get any good shots?" asked Cole, setting Zachary down on his feet.

Zachary clung to his fingers, teetering on his feet before letting go and taking a single step away.

Amber scooted toward Cole, settling beside him, scrolling her way through the pictures.

"Those are pretty good," said Cole.

"I can see now why he thinks you're familiar," she admitted. "It's absolutely there."

He turned to look at her. "You think?"

"I do."

Something clunked loudly on the floor, and they both looked up.

Zachary was clinging to the coffee table, slapping his palms against a puddle of eggnog while the glass rolled away.

"Oh, no," Amber groaned, quickly rising to her feet.

Otis immediately seized on the opportunity, jumping up to lap at the spilled eggnog.

"Otis, no," Cole commanded, following Amber. "This walking thing is going to take some getting used to."

The dog looked disappointed, but obediently went back to lie down.

Zachary stuffed his fingers into his mouth, breaking into a grin at the taste.

Amber reached for him, pulling the fingers free. "No rum for you, young man."

Cole gazed around. "You want me to take care of the baby or the mess?"

She felt a surge of gratitude for his offer. "Do you think you could give him a quick bath?"

"I'm on it." He took Zachary carefully into his arms, facing the messy parts away from his shirt and pants as he carried him down the hall. Otis followed along behind.

Sighing in resignation, Amber went to the kitchen storage room for paper towels and the mini steam cleaner.

Twenty minutes later, Cole's shirt was soaked through. But Zachary was clean and happy, tossing little plastic ducks around the tub. The kid had an arm, so some of the ducks flew across the purple bathroom. Cole wasn't about to leave Zachary's side, so they were running out of ducks.

"About done there, partner?" Cole asked, reaching forward to lift him.

Zachary grinned and kicked happily, sending a few final splashes toward Cole, one of them hitting him in the face and dampening his hair. Cole quickly wrapped Zachary's wiggly, wet body in a mauve towel, rubbing him dry before settling him on one hip. Then he leaned down to unplug the tub and used his free hand to gather up the errant ducks.

They made their way into the living room to find Amber on her hands and knees. The rumble and hiss of a steam-cleaning machine obscured the Christmas music. Her brow was sweaty, and her blouse was mussed as she pushed the appliance back and forth on the carpet.

She glanced up to see them. Then she rocked back, hitting the machine's off switch and swiping a hand across her forehead.

"I think I got it clean," she said.

Cole peeled his wet shirt away from his rib cage. "I'm not sure we've quite got the hang of this billionaire lifestyle."

She grinned. "He looks happy."

"He's happy. I'm soaking wet."

She came to her feet, dusting off her knees. "When it comes to babies, trust me, bathwater is the least of your problems."

"I'll keep that in mind."

"You want to take on diaper and pajama duty? Or do you want to put away the steamer?"

"Your choice. But after that, I want champagne and maybe some Belgium chocolate truffles sprinkled with gold flakes."

She shook her head in obvious confusion.

"Something billionaires would eat."

She moved to the wall to unplug the steamer. "That's a thing? Gold flakes on chocolate?"

"Real gold, apparently."

"And you eat it?"

"Well, I've never tried myself. But I hear tell it's expensive."

She coiled the cord. "Alright, Midas. You take diaper duty. I'll check the wine rack and pantry for things that are expensive."

"We can send out," he offered.

He didn't want her to go to any work. That was his whole point. Christmas Eve wasn't the time for cooking and cleaning.

"You're going to send out for gold chocolates?"

"For whatever you want."

"Let me see what we have first. And you might want to get the kid into a diaper before too long."

Cole glanced down at Zachary. "Right. Good advice."

Realizing the risk, he wasted no time in getting to the nursery. His diapering job was awkward but adequate, and he easily found a new pair of soft, stretchy pajamas.

Soon, they were back in the living room, then into the kitchen in search of Amber.

She turned from the counter, obviously hearing them arrive. "This brand comes in a wooden box and a gold bottle." She opened the lid of the champagne case to demonstrate. "It should be expensive enough to meet your standards."

"I was only joking."

She gave a shrug. "There's nobody around to drink it but us. And I don't think champagne keeps indefinitely."

The microwave oven beeped three times.

Amber pointed to the sound. "Zachary's Chateau Moo 2014 is in the microwave."

"Got it," said Cole, crossing the kitchen.

"We have fresh strawberries. And I found a few bars of dark chocolate. The label's in French, so I'm guessing they're imported. And this…"

Cole approached with the formula bottle in his hand.

"Gold-colored sugar sprinkles. Yellow, actually."

"You take me way too literally." But he couldn't help but be impressed by her ingenuity.

He perched himself on a stool, used his best guess on how to position Zachary and offered him the bottle.

Fortunately Zachary knew the drill. He snagged the bottle with both hands and relaxed into Cole's lap.

"I'm going to melt the chocolate, dip the strawberries and sprinkled them with gold."

"You clearly did not understand my point."

She blinked at him with a wide-eyed, ingenuous expression. "I thought you wanted gold-covered chocolate."

"Sure you did. I wanted luxury to come to us with no effort. That's how billionaires live."

She separated the halves of a double boiler, filling the bottom with water at the sink. "So far, for me anyway, the billionaire lifestyle is pretty much like any regular lifestyle. Except that it's a ridiculously long walk from the kitchen to the master bedroom. My tea is cold by the time I get there."

"You take tea to bed?"

"I sip jasmine while I read. It's very relaxing."

"I sip single malt while I watch the sports news. Very relaxing."

She lit a gas burner under the double boiler.

"You are actually making chocolate strawberries."

"It is Christmas Eve." Then a look of concern crossed her face. "Have you had dinner?"

"We grabbed a burger on the way over. You?"

"Late lunch."

"I really can order something in. You want a steak or some pasta? Or you seem to have a thing for pizza."

She pouted. "Okay, now you're making me hungry."

"Pizza it is." He paused, gazing down at Zachary. "I think this guy's out for the count."

Her expression softened, and she moved toward them. "I can take him if you'll watch the chocolate."

Cole extracted the bottle from Zachary's pursed mouth. He sucked a couple more times before sighing in his sleep.

"I've got him," he told her quietly. "I mean, if you're okay with me putting him to bed."

"Of course I'm okay with that." She brushed a hand across Zachary's forehead, then she followed it with a tender kiss.

Emotion tightened in Cole's chest. For the first time in his life, he actually got it. He'd seen men with their families, watched them care for their children. But he'd never had an inkling of the strength of those instincts, the flat-out intensity of the desire to protect.

"You sure?" he found himself asking.

He was little more than a stranger to Amber, and it suddenly seemed unfair to ask her to trust him with Zachary.

She smiled. "Go for it. Then order that pizza. We're going to need something that goes with five-hundred-dollar champagne."

"Is that seriously the price?" It struck Cole as ridiculous.

"That's what it says."

"How can any taste be worth twenty dollars a swallow?"

"You tell me. You're the billionaire."

Cole rose. "I guess we're about to find out."

He gently parked Zachary over his shoulder. Zachary's little body was warm and soft, molded trustingly in his arms.

Minutes later, he finished tucking Zachary into his crib, leaving Otis posted across the open doorway, and returned to the kitchen to find Amber with a dozen chocolate-dipped strawberries lined up on waxed paper. She was sprinkling "gold" on the sticky chocolate.

"I'm impressed," he told her, coming up behind her.

"They turned out pretty good." She sounded happy, and that made him smile.

The scent of chocolate and strawberries floated around them. Her hair brushed his arm. He knew he was standing too close, but he hadn't the slightest desire to move.

He wanted to touch her, to wrap his arms around her, kiss the back of her neck, then turn her around and kiss her mouth. Forget the strawberries, he wanted to strip her naked and make love to her all night long.

"I was thinking a pesto pizza," she said. "Maybe with mushrooms and dried tomatoes, nothing too overpowering."

"Whatever you want," said Cole, realizing he meant it in every sense of the word.

"And feta cheese?"

He could see the corner of her widening grin. "Why is that funny?"

"Makes it more expensive."

"Now you're catching on. We'll definitely get some feta."

It was time to step back. It was time for him to step back from Amber and call a pizza place. He drew a deep breath to brace himself, telling his feet to get a move on. But he inhaled her scent above the strawberries.

And then she turned. She turned, and she was right there, in front of him, her lips only inches away.

"Do you want to change out of your wet clothes?" she asked. "There might be something around here of Samuel's that—"

"No." The question was like a bucket of cold water. "I'm not wearing Samuel's clothes."

Amber looked slightly hurt. "Okay."

"I'm sorry. He wasn't good to my mother, but it's a long story." Cole extracted his phone. "I'll order the pizza."

"You don't want to talk about it."

He didn't. Then again, it wasn't some big, painful secret that he couldn't discuss.

Samuel was a jerk who never deserved Lauren's love. But Cole wasn't going to waste any emotional energy hating the man, either. He didn't care. And he hadn't cared for a very long time. There was no reason not to tell Amber the story.

"I'm fine to talk about it. But let's pour the champagne first."

Eleven

They were on their second glass of champagne, munching their way through the pizza before Amber asked him again.

"You don't mind telling me about Samuel?"

She was at one end of the sofa, Cole at the other. She'd turned sideways to face him, crossing her legs beneath her. His body was canted sideways, one leg up on the leather cushion.

"There's nothing much to tell. You know I never met him. All I know is what my mother told me."

"Did she hate him?" From what little Cole had said, Amber guessed his mother, Lauren, had gotten a very raw deal.

"She hated his weakness, that he caved to his family." Cole stretched an arm along the back of the sofa. "They fell quickly and deeply in love. But she didn't come from the right family, hadn't been to the right schools, didn't have the refined tastes and manners he knew his parents would look for in a daughter-in-law. So he married her without telling them, thinking once it was a done deal, his parents would be forced to accept her."

"They didn't," Amber guessed.

"They went ballistic. They ordered him to divorce her right away, and to never admit to anyone that she'd existed. If he didn't, they said they'd disinherit him. No surprise that he loved the family money more than he loved my mother."

"He didn't deserve her," Amber said softly.

"I must have said that to her ten thousand times."

Cole fell silent, looking sad, and Amber found her heart going out to him. "You don't have to talk about it."

"He was nothing to me. I mean, nothing. I was angry off and on, especially as a teenager. But then I realized he didn't even deserve my anger. As far as I was concerned, he might as well have not existed. When he died…"

Cole lifted the crystal flute and took a drink of his champagne. "This sounds terrible, but when he died, I didn't care. I knew I should. But I didn't. I wasn't sad. I wasn't glad. I didn't expect his death or anything about the Henderson family to be even a blip on my life. Things were going to carry on as normal."

"It didn't occur to you there might be an inheritance?"

"Not even for a second."

She set down her half-eaten slice of pizza, exchanging it for the glass of champagne. "So why did you come to Atlanta?"

"Luca kept after me. Then one day, I gave in. I looked at a picture of Zachary. I don't know. There was something about him, something in his eyes. I knew I had to at least make sure he was safe and secure."

Amber's chest tingled and went tight. "You came here to take care of your brother."

"And then I met you." The look in his eyes was tender. "And I knew Zachary was safe. It was just a matter of getting through the hearing without anyone figuring out who I was."

"But then I lost."

He nodded. "I didn't know what to do. I'd learned enough about Roth by then that I couldn't let him win."

"Thank you."

"There's no need to thank me. And I haven't defeated him yet."

"But you're trying. You really don't want Coast Eagle, do you?"

"I want what's best for Zachary. It's ironic, really. When I first heard about him, I resented him. All I could think was that he was going to have the easy life while Mom and I had struggled so hard to get by."

Amber set down her glass, impulsively shifting closer. "But now you care."

He gazed into her eyes. "It's pretty easy to care."

She reached for his hands and squeezed. "It's pretty easy to care about you, too, Cole."

She'd meant to be reassuring, friendly and comforting. But her tone had become breathy, and the atmosphere thickened between them.

Cole stroked his thumbs across the backs of her hands. Then he stroked the inside of her wrists, watching as he moved his way up her bare arm.

Arousal became a deep, base pulse in the center of her body.

He raised his head, and there was a tremor in his tone. "I know I have no right to ask."

She wanted him to ask. She desperately wanted him to ask.

"Just for tonight," he said. "Just for a little while."

She nodded.

"Can we stop fighting it?"

She nodded harder.

"Oh, Amber." He leaned forward, placing his lips against hers, tenderly at first, but then with unmistakable purpose. She came up on her knees, wrapped her arms around his neck, pulling forward to kiss him more deeply.

He turned her into his lap, his hand splaying across her stomach as his tongue teased hers.

Instinct took over, and her body arched reflexively toward him while their kiss continued.

"You are so beautiful," he breathed.

"You are so wet." She drew back to stare at his shirtfront. "You're still soaking wet."

He gave a soft chuckle. "I could take it off."

"Yes." She nodded, pretending it was merely a practical suggestion. "You should take it off."

He flipped the buttons open, making his way down the pale gray shirt. She glimpsed his chest, then his abs. Then he peeled the shirt away, revealing his muscular shoulders and arms. He was an incredibly magnificent man.

"You're the one who's beautiful," she told him.

She gifted a lingering kiss on his smooth chest, flicking out her tongue to leave a wetter spot on his skin.

"Do that again." His voice was tight.

She kissed him again, tasting the salt of his skin, feeling his heat through the tenderness of her lips.

"I got your shirt wet," he rasped.

"That's too bad." She kissed a slow path across his chest.

One of his hands bracketed her hip; the other undid the buttons on her shirt.

"Are you fixing it?" she asked, lips brushing his skin as she spoke.

"I'm fixing it."

"That's good." She shrugged out of the shirt, revealing her white lace bra.

"All good." He released the catch on her bra, peeling it off. "All very, very good."

She knew she should be self-conscious, even embarrassed by her nakedness in the well-lit living room.

"If Destiny and Luca come back, we're…" She moved up to kiss his neck, bracing her hands on his shoulders, absorbing the feel of their taut texture.

"Oh, darling," he drawled. "They're not coming back."

"They're not?" Not that she was truly worried. She wasn't about to stop undressing Cole.

"Did you see their expressions?" There was a chuckle in his voice. "They're not coming back."

She unsnapped the top of his fly. "Just as well."

His warm hand closed over her breast. "I like the way you're thinking."

She bit back a moan. "What am I thinking?"

"That you want me." He narrowed his attention to her nipple.

A zing of sensation flashed to the apex of her thighs, and this time she did moan. "I do want you."

"I want you, too, very, very badly."

She wrapped her arms around his neck, bringing her mouth to his. "Oh, Cole."

"Amber." He tunneled his spread fingers into her hair, kissing her deeper and deeper.

She fumbled with her pants, while he got rid of his.

Then she was lying back on the sofa, pulling him to her, impatient and anxious to become one. But he made her wait, feathering his fingertips along her thighs, circling and teasing as he went.

"Now," she begged.

"Yeah?" he asked, his voice husky, breathing deep.

"Right now." The anticipation was too much.

"In a hurry?"

She knew how to stop this game. She raked her fingertips down his stomach, going lower until she grasped him, wrapping her hand smoothly around his length.

His body convulsed. "Okay."

"In a hurry?" she managed.

"Yes." He disentangled her hand, drawing her arms up above her head. "I'm definitely in a hurry."

Moments later, he was inside her, swift and sure, and she gasped at the strength of the sensations. His movements were steady and deep. Her reaction more and more intense.

He kissed her mouth, his hand going to her breast. She was bombarded with pleasure over every inch of her body. Time seemed to stop while she drank in his taste, scent and touch. She never wanted it to end.

"You're amazing." His lips brushed hers as he spoke. "I've never...ever...ever..."

"Cole," she gasped. "Don't stop. Please don't stop."

"I'm never stopping. Not...ever."

But she could feel it. She could feel her climax shimmering. Her body climbed higher and higher, her nerves extending, muscles tightening, until it all crashed into an apex of pleasure.

She cried out.

He groaned her name.

And their bodies peaked as one.

She was weightless at first, then exhausted, her limbs too heavy to move.

"That was your fault," he muttered in her ear.

It took her a moment to muster up the energy to speak. "What was my fault?"

"You ended it."

"I did. You're just too good."

"Oh, darling. That was exactly what I wanted to hear."

She cautiously blinked her eyes open, the twinkling Christmas tree coming into focus, then the fireplace and the champagne bottle.

Cole's weight pressed her into the sofa. For the first time in what seemed like forever, she felt safe, content and at home.

Cole eased himself into the giant tub in the master bathroom, settling at the end opposite to Amber. He'd lit candles all around and set the champagne glasses and the rest of the bottle on the wide tiled edge. The water was steaming in billows toward the box window that overlooked the city, mingling with the scent of citrus that filled the air.

"This *is* practically a pool," he couldn't help but note, stretching his arms to each side, his legs brushing lightly against Amber's beneath the water.

Amber lifted her champagne flute. "Are we behaving like billionaires now?"

Her hair was swept up in a messy knot. Her cheeks were flushed, her lips dark red and her lashes thick against the crystal blue of her eyes. Her breasts bobbed ever so slightly beneath the surface of the water. She had the most beautiful breasts he'd ever seen.

"Close enough," he answered. "I've got everything in the world I want right here."

She smiled. "Plus gold chocolates in the kitchen."

"I forgot about those."

She gave a mock frown.

"I mean," he said, attempting to properly appreciate her efforts, "I can't wait to try one."

She raised her glass in a mock toast. "Now you're catching on."

He drank with her. "So tell me what you have planned for tomorrow."

She looked puzzled. "Tomorrow?"

"Christmas Day."

Her expression said that she'd completely forgotten the date. He was going to take that as a positive sign.

"Presents for Zachary," she said. "And Destiny's coming

over. Luca, too, maybe? And…" This time a flash of worry creased her face.

"What?" he asked.

She shook her head.

"Something upset you. What was it?"

"Uh, you guys didn't…"

He wasn't following, and he gave his head a little shake.

She gestured to her naked body. "Please tell me you two didn't plan…this."

The question shocked him so much, it took several seconds to form an answer. "No."

Admittedly, it wasn't the most comprehensive answer in the world. He tried again. "We didn't plan a thing. Okay, yes, I know that Luca likes Destiny. And I guess he knows I like you. But we never talked about sex, and we sure as hell didn't plan out some Christmas Eve seduction scenario." Frankly, he was a little insulted by her suggestion.

"You don't talk to Luca about sex?"

Her question was so genuine that Cole's annoyance disappeared. "I don't talk to him about sex with you."

"Oh." She shifted under the water, looking decidedly guilty.

Wait a minute. "You talked about *me* with Destiny."

Amber blushed. "She asked me."

"And you told her?" He pretended to be affronted, but it was a struggle not to laugh.

"Sorry," she offered faintly.

He polished off his glass of champagne. "I'm the one who's sorry. I'm just messing with you. Tell anybody you want."

"I only told Destiny."

He gave a shrug as he reached for the champagne bottle. "I honestly don't care. But I won't tell Luca anything that makes you uncomfortable."

He gestured with the bottle.

She held out her glass. "I know it seems like the double standard."

"It *is* a double standard. But me and the rest of the male population have come to terms with it."

"Now I feel guilty."

"Don't. Believe me when I tell you, guilt is the last thing I'm going for here."

She seemed to relax and leaned back against the edge of the tub. "What exactly are you going for?"

"I have to say, I enjoyed the part where you said I was too good at sex." He paused. "And I liked the expression on your face when you said it. And I liked that I was holding you in my arms at the time. And that you were naked."

Arousal reawakened as he spoke.

He couldn't seem to get enough of looking at her, talking to her, touching her. But it was close to midnight, and he knew this interlude had to end—likely very soon.

"Come here," he told her softly.

Her blue eyes went wide in obvious surprise.

He set his glass aside. "Come sit with me."

It took her a minute to react. But then she braced herself on the edge of the tub and slipped across, candles flickering in the mist as she settled between his legs. The glass of champagne was still in her hand.

He wrapped his arms around her stomach, holding her naked softness to his body and kissed the crook of her neck. Her supple warmth, smooth skin and the subtle scent of her shampoo brought back memories of their lovemaking. He wanted her all over again.

"Tell me about Alaska," she said, relaxing against him.

"It's cold."

"How incredibly informative."

"Lots of snow, mountains, wildlife. The people are amazing. There's no road access to Juneau, so there's a very close-knit sense of community."

"You have no roads?"

"We have roads in the city, of course. But the only way to get there from the mainland is by ferry, boat or airplane. Good for business at Aviation 58."

"Is there much there? Can you shop?"

"We have stores, groceries, clothes, hardware, even car dealerships, certainly everything you need for day-to-day life. There are over thirty thousand people living in Juneau."

"That's less than a football game."

"That's why we have such a great sense of community."

"What do you do up there?"

"Mostly, I run a business and fly airplanes."

"And for fun?"

"Ski, snowmobile, mountain climb, swim, soccer. There's plenty of outdoor recreation, but we also have plays, music, restaurants, movie theatres, even fashion shows."

"Just like a regular city."

"Exactly like a regular city. But with more snow and more bears."

"I'd be terrified of bears."

"They're not exactly walking down the main drag in Juneau." He paused. "Well, not often."

"Are you serious? Or are you messing with me again?"

"It's rare. But it can happen. You should come and check it out."

As soon as the words were out, he felt the shift in atmosphere. He could have kicked himself. He and Amber were, right this moment, a tiny oasis in the midst of their bizarre situation.

"I'm sorry," he offered.

"It's okay."

"No, it's not. I didn't mean to hint we were going somewhere as a couple. That's just insincere and misleading, even manipulative."

Her tone went cool. "Don't worry, Cole. I won't be dropping in on you in Alaska."

"That's not what I meant, either. I'd love to have you come to Alaska."

Her body was growing stiffer by the second. "Isn't this where we came into this conversation?"

"I'm so sorry."

He smoothed back her hair. He couldn't help himself, he kissed her dewy neck. When she didn't rebuff him, he kissed her jawline. Then he tipped back her head and kissed her mouth.

The second he tasted her, arousal hijacked his senses. He kissed her deeply, turning her in his arms until she was facing him, straddling his lap, her wet breasts sliding along his chest. He sat up straight. He cupped her bottom, pulling her tight to the V of his legs.

He was right where he wanted to be. But the water was cooling off, and they were going to have to leave soon.

"I don't want to hurt you," he whispered.

"You're not."

"I want the world to go away. I want to stay right here and forget everything else. I don't want to let you go."

She nodded.

"Amber. You're incredible." He cradled her face, kissing her all over again.

Then he drew back, and they gazed at each other for a long, long time.

"Can I stay tonight?" he dared ask.

"I want you to stay."

His heart swelled with satisfaction, and he folded her into his arms.

Christmas morning, it wasn't clear to Amber which delighted Zachary more, ripping into presents or walking across the room on his own. He had no interest at all in any of the toys, but wandered from chair to table to ottoman with ribbons and bows in hands.

Otis stayed off to one side, looking stoic and long-suffering when Zachary grabbed at his fur or ears or tried to decorate him.

A few hours ago, Cole had had the presence of mind to put his clothes through the laundry. So while he was dressed the same as last night, the clothes, at least, were fresh.

Amber had given her hair a blow dry this morning, put on a little more makeup than usual and dressed in a pair of skinny black slacks and a shimmering red blouse. She'd chosen a funky pair of Christmas-ball earrings and felt überfestive. She had to admit, it was nice to have Cole around to entertain Zachary while she had spent the extra time getting ready.

Destiny arrived with Luca midmorning, and neither seemed surprised to find Cole on the floor with Zachary.

A couple of wrapped gifts in his hands, Luca headed for the tree. Destiny grasped Amber's arm to hold her back.

"Tell me what happened," she whispered in Amber's ear.

Amber pretended she didn't understand the question. "When?"

Destiny rolled her eyes. "Last night."

"What happened with you last night? I thought you'd come back."

"We had a great time, that's what happened with me."

"Great?" Amber asked. "Or *great?*"

Cole offered Luca a cup of coffee, and the two, along with Zachary and Otis, headed for the kitchen.

"Both," Destiny answered as the men disappeared. "We toured the lights, had a few drinks and went back to his hotel."

Amber filled in the blank. "And that's all she wrote?"

"I'm hoping we'll write some more."

Amber grinned and gave Destiny a one-armed hug as they moved into the living room.

"And you?" Destiny asked, brows going up as they each took a seat.

"Cole stayed the night."

"So it's better? You've made up?"

"*Made up* is not the right phrase. We didn't, don't have a relationship."

"What is it you have?"

Amber thought back to Cole's words last night in the tub. "I don't know. A mutual problem?"

"That doesn't sound very romantic."

Maybe not, but Amber was determined to see it for what it was and enjoy it for what it was. Last night with Cole had been amazing, and this morning had been fun. There was no point in speculating beyond that.

"You want coffee?" she asked Destiny.

"Please."

As Amber rose, she heard a phone ring from inside the

kitchen and recognized it as Cole's. Destiny followed behind her into the kitchen and took a seat at the island counter, where Zachary was in his high chair playing with a little pile of breakfast cereal rounds.

"When?" Cole asked into the phone. His tone was serious, and he gave a sideways glance to Amber.

She instantly knew something was wrong.

She glanced reflexively at Zachary, grateful he was right here beside her where she could see he was fine.

"How many?" Cole asked.

Amber found herself moving toward him.

He reached out and put a hand on her shoulder.

"Are you sure?" He paused. "Hundred percent?" He breathed a sigh. "Yeah. I will. You've got it. Call me if you hear anything else."

"What is it?" Amber asked, holding her breath.

"There was another hydraulic problem with a Boonsome 300."

Her tone went hushed. "The same thing?"

Cole nodded. "Astra Airlines. The flight was coming into O'Hare."

"Has it landed?" She swallowed. She couldn't bring herself to use the word *crashed*.

"Belly landing onto foam. Everyone got out, but there was a fire. The plane's destroyed. The federal government has grounded the Boonsomes, and they need complete access to the Coast Eagle plane at LAX."

"Absolutely," said Amber. "Whatever they need."

She stopped speaking and sucked in gulps of air, her mind galloping to what-if scenarios. What if she hadn't grounded the Coast Eagle fleet? Her decision had been based on her gut feeling, not on any technical expertise. She was an accountant, not an aviation specialist. What if she'd made the wrong choice, and a Coast Eagle flight had crashed and killed the passengers?

She felt the room spin around her, and a wave of nausea cramped her stomach.

Cole's hand tightened on her shoulder. "Amber?"

She pushed him off and bolted for the living room.

She made it as far as the hallway, and gripped the corner of the wall to steady herself.

Cole was instantly behind her, his hands on her shoulders.

"They're all okay." His tone was soothing. "Bumps and bruises, maybe a couple of cracked ribs. The captain did a spectacular job on the landing."

She swallowed the lump in her throat. "What if I hadn't?" she managed.

"Hadn't what?" He came around to look at her.

"What if I hadn't grounded the Coast Eagle fleet?"

"But you did. You made exactly the right decision."

"Because I listened to you."

"You listened to everyone in the room, and then you made the call."

"I'm scared, Cole," she admitted, starting to shake. "I'm not qualified to do this. I shouldn't be cochair of Coast Eagle. Nobody should be listening to me."

He drew her into his arms and smoothed a hand over her hair. "If they'd listened to Roth, a Coast Eagle plane might very well have crashed."

Amber digested that thought. She knew there had to be a counterargument to it, but she couldn't come up with it right now.

"They'll find the problem," said Cole, the certainty in his deep voice making her feel unaccountably better. "They'll fix it, and nobody else is going to get hurt."

"I want to go back to my regular job."

He looked down at her and gave her a smile. "You'd abandon me?"

"You made the right decision, right off, because of your knowledge and experience."

"Amber, the single most important attribute of being a good decision maker is listening—listening to the right people and weighing all the evidence. Nobody is an expert in everything. That's Roth's downfall. He won't listen to anyone but himself."

She had to concede that was true.

"It's Christmas," said Cole, rubbing her upper arms. "Everyone is safe, and the right people are out there doing their jobs. Let's take one more day to forget about the chaos all around us. Can we have one more day for us?"

She forced herself to break away from him. He was right. This was Zachary's first Christmas, and there was nothing that needed her immediate attention.

"Yes," she told him.

"Good. We should get outside for a while. Do you think Zachary would like a walk in the park?"

Amber knew Zachary would love a walk in the park. And so would she. Cole's instincts seemed bang on when it came to the two of them.

Twelve

By the time the judge called a recess, Cole could feel his blood pressure pounding inside his ears. Over Destiny's continued objections, Roth's lawyer had painted Cole as a conniving, opportunistic fortune hunter who had deliberately kept himself hidden from the Henderson family until there was some profit for him. The man had scoffed at the idea that Cole hadn't known about the will. And he'd railed about the unfairness of placing Zachary in the care of a man that neither of his parents had ever met.

It had taken all of Cole's self-control to stay quiet and seated. Now he shot up from his seat and rushed from the courtroom, keeping his gaze straight ahead as he passed through the gallery. He needed to bring his anger under control before he spoke with anyone.

He took long strides through the foyer, out onto the sidewalk, turning down the block where he could disappear into the crowd. He drew long breaths of the crisp air, trying desperately to clear his rioting emotions.

"Mr. Henderson?" a voice called from behind.

Cole didn't turn. The last thing in the world he needed right now was another nosey reporter. He wove through the busy sidewalks, lengthening his stride to put some distance between them.

"Mr. Henderson?" the voice repeated.

Cole took two more paces then decided to put an end to the intrusion. He pivoted, spread his feet and clenched his fists by his sides. "Do you mind—"

"Sorry to bother you. I'm Kevin Kent, president of Cambridge Airlines." The fiftysomething man huffed as he caught up.

The introduction surprised Cole.

"We're based out of London, England," said the man, holding out a business card.

Cole didn't take it. He didn't want to talk to anyone, not a reporter, not an airline executive, not Destiny, not anyone.

"Is there something I can do for you?" he snarled.

The traffic rolled past them, echoing against the pavement, while groups of pedestrians parted to go around.

"I've been watching the proceedings in the courtroom."

Cole didn't respond to the statement. The courtroom had been packed for a day and half, with a lineup outside. It seemed most of the city was watching the proceedings.

"I know you're taking a beating, but my money's on you."

If Kevin Kent wanted a thank-you for the vote of confidence, he was going to be disappointed.

"I've spent some time looking into your Alaska holdings," he continued. "Do you have a second to talk?"

"Here? Now? You want to talk about *Alaska?*" Who cared about Alaska? Zachary's future was on the line.

The man glanced at the multistory buildings around them. "There's a coffee shop on the corner."

"I'm not on a coffee break."

"Right. Okay. I'll get to it. I know you have a thriving airline in Alaska. That you built it from the ground up, and you have a partner and friend in that business with you."

Cole was getting impatient. So Kevin Kent could do an internet search. Big deal.

"When this court case ends, if you win, you're going to have a big decision to make."

Cole crossed his arms over his chest. No kidding. What else had the man deduced?

"I'm banking on you winning," said Kevin. "And I'm banking on your loyalty to Aviation 58."

"Are you working up to a point, Mr. Kent?"

"Call me Kevin. Yes. My point is you may be in the market to sell."

Cole drew back. "Sell Aviation 58?" There wasn't a chance in hell he'd sell his airline.

"No," said Kevin. "Coast Eagle Airlines."

Cole felt the ground shift beneath him; he dropped his arms to steady himself. The bustle of the downtown street went momentarily still and silent. "Sell Coast Eagle?"

"To Cambridge Airlines."

Cole wasn't sure he'd heard right. He was trying to save Coast Eagle for Zachary's future.

"I'm not in the market to sell," he assured Kevin. "I won't *be* in the market to sell."

"Perhaps not." Kevin seemed to be watching Cole closely. "Though I'm not sure you've had an opportunity to think through the complexities of running two separate airlines."

"I'm not going to—" Cole caught himself.

He hadn't thought of it in those terms. But if he won the custody battle, who *would* run Coast Eagle? He wasn't staying in Atlanta. He'd never planned to stay in Atlanta.

Max had made it clear he was temporary as president, and he wasn't the right fit anyway. Roth was absolutely not going to be in charge. Sidney was smart, but new to the VP post. Cole's take was that he needed several years of mentoring before taking on more responsibility.

"We have the corporate depth," said Kevin. "And we have the expertise. You'd have the choice to remain as a minor shareholder, of course. I won't lie to you, I think that would be a good investment. But we'd prefer to buy you out. Have you looked into Coast Eagle's net worth?"

Cole had not. Things had been moving ahead so quickly that he hadn't focused any attention at all on what happened after the court case. And at the moment, he was a lot more worried about the possibility of losing than of winning.

"You need to think about it," Kevin told him softly. "I'm not being opportunistic, and I'd fully expect due diligence on your side. But my take is that you need to win this. And my take is that you're going to fight with everything you've got. And when you win, I want to talk. Because I think you're going to have to make a choice—Coast Eagle or Aviation 58."

He offered his card again. "Call me anytime."

This time, Cole took the card. Kevin Kent gave him a nod and walked away.

Afterward, Cole stood still for a full five minutes.

How could he possibly sell Coast Eagle? Then again, how on earth was he going to run it?

"Mr. Henderson?"

Cole gave himself a mental shake.

This time the man who approached him was a reporter. "Frank Hast, Atlanta Weekly. How do you respond to the accusation that you're using your half brother as a pawn to get your hands on the Henderson fortune?"

Cole stared at the man, wondering what would happen if he simply slammed him into a wall.

"I don't," he said instead and began walking away.

The reporter paced alongside. "Then what do you say to reports that you're using a relationship with Amber Welsley to undermine Roth Calvin?"

The word *relationship* stopped Cole in his tracks. He almost rose to the bait, but he checked himself just in time. "Roth Calvin needs to worry about the facts, not about anything I have to say."

"What *is* your relationship with Amber Welsley?"

"Ms. Welsley is the guardian of my half brother."

"For the moment."

Cole began walking again.

"One more question, Mr. Henderson."

"I have to get back to court."

"But—"

Cole lengthened his stride.

The man hustled to catch up. "Do you agree that Roth Calvin was wrong to put profit before passengers' lives?"

Cole was tempted to answer that one, but he held his tongue and kept going. He was saving his arguments for the judge. The reporter finally gave up.

Luca was on the steps of the courthouse as Cole approached. He quickly spotted Cole and came forward to meet him.

"You okay?" he asked, glancing around as if gauging their distance from possible eavesdroppers.

"Not really."

Luca nodded his understanding. "Destiny was looking for you."

"I needed some air."

"Yeah."

Their conversation ended, but Cole's mind was clicking its way through information and options.

"Have you given any thought to what happens after?" he asked Luca.

"If you lose?"

"If I win."

Luca cocked his head. "No. And honestly, I don't think that's what you need to worry about right now."

"Maybe not," Cole allowed. They were a very long way from winning. But Kevin Kent had gotten him thinking.

"You're the underdog," said Luca.

Cole blew out a breath, telling himself to focus. "What did Destiny want?"

"To talk strategy."

"Are we changing it?" Cole didn't think that was a bad idea. They had hoped Cole's blood connection to Zachary would be their trump card, since the courts overwhelmingly sided with family. But Roth's attack on Cole's motivations and character had clearly turned the tide against them.

"She wants to demonstrate that Roth's sole interest in Zachary is his stake in Coast Eagle."

"So far, he's the one doing that to me."

"He's never spent any time with Zachary."

"Neither had I until last week." Cole knew he was sounding pessimistic. But he was feeling pessimistic.

Luca glanced at his watch. "She thinks it's the best bet."

Cole didn't think it was a huge strength. But they were running out of time and out of options. "I wish I had something better."

"So do I," said Luca. "We have to go back."

"And after?" asked Cole.

"Don't think about it."

"I have to think about it."

"Let's get through today. Whatever happens, we'll face it tomorrow."

Cole gave a reluctant nod. The best thing he could do for Zachary was to remain focused for the rest of the afternoon. If they got a decision today, whichever way it went, they'd start working through their next options in the morning.

Though the courtroom was packed, it was surprisingly quiet. From the third row, Amber focused on Cole's posture. His shoulders were tense, his body completely still as Roth's lawyer gave his summation.

"Samuel Henderson made his final wishes clear," the man's voice boomed with authority. "He named Roth Calvin as his son and heir's legal guardian. Samuel Henderson has known Roth Calvin for over a decade. He has put his trust in Roth Calvin." He made a half turn and pointed to Cole. "Nobody, not this man or anybody else, has the right to undermine Samuel Henderson's wishes on such an important, intimate and fundamental decision of who would raise his son in the event of his death. There is no ambiguity here, Your Honor."

As his voice thundered on, Amber's heart thudded harder. Sweat broke out on her palms. This was hopeless.

They were going to lose.

She was absolutely positive they were going to lose.

The room seemed suddenly hot, and her stomach churned with nausea. She rose from her seat. She could feel Luca watching her as she rushed to the back of the gallery, bursting through the double doors and heading for the ladies' room.

The length of the lobby felt endless, but finally she made it into the cool quiet of the restroom. She gripped the counter, staring at her reflection in the mirror, tears stinging her eyes as she willed her stomach to calm down. She didn't have time to fall apart.

"Think," she ordered herself. *"Think!"*

The marble counter was cold and hard, and her hands started to ache from the pressure of her grip. She ran through every wild and crazy solution, including grabbing Zachary and making a run for it.

Then, in a rush, it came to her fully formed. It was crazy. And it was a gamble, a huge gamble that might very well backfire on her. But at least it was something.

She let go of the counter and retrieved her cell phone from her purse. Then she pressed the speed-dial button for the penthouse.

It was silent, then it clicked, then silence again.

"Come on, come on, come on."

Roth's lawyer was probably finishing up, and there was only so much Destiny had to say.

Finally, the call rang through.

"Welsley-Henderson residence."

"Isabel?"

"Amber? Did they—"

"No. Not yet. But I need you to do something for me. And I need you to do it right now. It's important, and you have to hurry."

"Certainly, ma'am."

"Bring Zachary to the courthouse."

"He's asleep."

"I don't care. Wake him up. Don't stop to change him or to feed him. Tell the driver to go as fast as humanly possible. I'll meet you out front."

"But—"

"Just do it. There's not a second to waste."

"Okay," said Isabel. "Yes. I will."

Amber shut off her phone and tucked it away. She took a final, bracing breath, staring back at her reflection. This might be the stupidest move she'd ever pulled. But she didn't see any other possible hope. If she didn't do something, they'd lose.

She settled her purse strap on her shoulder. Then she left the restroom and made her way back across the big foyer. Her footfalls echoed against the high ceiling and the marble pillars. Sunlight streamed through a wall of glass above the main doors.

It was far too early to go outside to meet Isabel, but she was too jumpy to sit back down in the gallery. She stopped outside the courtroom. She cautiously cracked the door open and saw Destiny come to her feet. All she could hope was that Destiny had a lot to rebut.

She let the door swing shut again and began pacing in the opposite direction. She took a curved staircase to the second floor, walked the perimeter, then took the staircase back down again. She wandered through a side hallway and found an ancillary exit. She took it and walked the three blocks around the complex to the front courthouse stairs.

There she stood, telling herself it was still too early to expect Isabel and Zachary, but scrutinizing every dark sedan that came into view from the south.

She checked her watch. Fifteen minutes had passed.

"Come on, Isabel."

Another five minutes, maybe three minutes, and she'd let herself call Isabel's cell.

And then she spotted the dark blue sedan with Harrison at the wheel. She rushed to the curb, meeting it as it came to a stop, grabbing the back passenger-side handle.

It was locked. Her hand snapped away, and she had to steady herself.

"Ms. Welsley?" Harrison called, rising to look at her over the top of the car.

"Unlock," she called. "I have to hurry."

"Of course, ma'am."

The lock clicked, and Amber pulled open the door. She went to work on the car seat harness, tugging it free, releasing Zachary's arms and legs.

He blinked up at her, sleepy, puzzled.

"Is something wrong?" asked Isabel.

"I'm in a rush," Amber answered, pulling Zachary against her shoulder and stepping back. "They're almost finished."

She turned.

"The diaper bag," Isabel called after her.

"No time," Amber tossed over her shoulder, running up the stairs.

Zachary whimpered in her ear.

She didn't blame him. Poor little thing, dragged unceremoniously out of his bed, probably tired and hungry, likely with a very wet diaper.

"I'm sorry, sweetheart," she whispered in his ear. "But I have to try. I *have* to try."

She pulled open the door, still at a jog as she crossed the far-too-large foyer.

Zachary's whimpers become more insistent as she swung open the courtroom door.

Destiny was on her feet, back to the gallery, talking to the judge. "The precedent Chamber versus Hathaway clearly applies and clearly demonstrates..."

Amber's footsteps slowed as she experienced a rush of unadulterated fear. Was this stupid? Was she making a mistake? But then she focused on the back of Cole's head and forced herself to move forward.

Zachary started to squirm in her arms. His whimpers were turning into whines.

Luca stared at her as she passed the third row. But she ignored him. She ignored the stares of the spectators, and even the curious brow raise from the judge. She moved rudely in front of three people in the front row.

"Cole," she hissed. "Cole?"

He turned, and his expression faltered. "What's wrong?"

At the sound of Cole's voice, Zachary instantly swung around. He howled and lunged for him. As Cole had done a dozen times, he neatly reached out and caught Zachary in his arms.

Destiny turned, and then everything focused on the commotion.

"Order," called the judge, banging his gavel.

Zachary's arms wrapped tight around Cole's neck, and he buried his sobbing face against the crook of Cole's neck.

Destiny moved toward the pair. "Your Honor, this is Zachary Henderson."

The judge peered over the top of his glasses. "I will not allow this hearing to turn into a circus."

But Zachary's sobs were already subsiding, his little body relaxing against Cole's chest.

Roth's lawyer came to his feet. "Objection, Your Honor."

The judge swung his attention to the defendant's table. "What grounds are you going to choose?"

"The plaintiff is not permitted to use props."

"Props?" asked Destiny, with exactly the right note of surprise and censure in her tone.

"Props," the man repeated. "The plaintiff clearly believes that holding Zachary Henderson will make him look to the court like the more capable guardian."

"Mr. Henderson is the more capable guardian." Destiny nudged Cole. "However, if Mr. Calvin would rather hold the prop himself, we have no objection." She looked hard at Cole.

Cole was quick to pick up on the message, walking straight over to Roth to offer Zachary.

Roth jumped to his feet.

"Here you go," said Cole, holding the soggy Zachary out toward him.

As Roth recoiled, Zachary shrieked in obvious terror, reaching desperately for Cole.

"No?" Cole said to Roth.

He pulled poor Zachary back against his chest.

Zachary clung there, breaths shuddering in and out while murmurs came up all across the courtroom.

Destiny jumped back in. "In the interest of peace and order, I'd suggest we let Mr. Henderson hold his brother."

The other lawyer glared at her.

The judge banged his gavel.

Destiny turned to Amber. "Give me your phone. Quick."

Amber scrambled for her phone, handing it over to Destiny.

Cole sat down, and Zachary went mercifully quiet.

"Excuse me, miss?" A woman whispered behind Amber.

Amber turned to find the woman had scooted down to make room on the bench. She patted the spot.

Amber smiled her thanks and sat down.

Nobody seemed certain of what to do next, but Destiny spoke right up, talking while she glanced up and down from the tiny screen on Amber's phone. "Since arriving in Atlanta," she spoke loud and clearly to the judge, "Mr. Henderson has forged a special and intimate bond with his brother."

"Objection," said the other lawyer. "Their purported relationship is no more than hearsay. And it's his half brother."

Destiny glanced meaningfully down at Zachary cuddled up to Cole, obviously letting everyone make up their own mind about the relationship between the two.

"I'll rephrase," she said. "Since arriving in Atlanta, Mr. Henderson has spent a great deal of time with his baby *half* brother. This includes babysitting, feeding, bathing, diapering, playing with him and many hours of cuddling Zachary. In fact, Mr. Henderson spent Christmas Eve and Christmas Day with his half brother."

She took three paces to a small computer table. "I'd like to introduce into evidence some photographs." She swiftly plugged a cord into Amber's phone.

Amber couldn't help but smile.

Immediately, the picture of Cole and Zachary under the Christmas tree came up. Zachary looked adoringly up at Cole as he grasped Cole's nose, grinning. The expression on Cole's face was tender and loving.

"Objection," said Roth's lawyer.

As Destiny turned to acknowledge the lawyer's request, she obviously pressed a button on the phone. A candid shot came up, Zachary and Cole romping with Otis. It was even better than the first.

"On what grounds?" asked the judge.

"The plaintiff is clearly using these photos as a tool of manipulation. They're staged."

"They're family Christmas photos," said the judge. "Since

Christmas Day took place last week, I have no reason to doubt the voracity of the photographs."

Destiny immediately brought up the next photo. It was Cole holding Zachary wrapped in a fluffy towel. The baby was clearly fresh from the bath, and gazed happily into Cole's eyes.

Amber's heart warmed at the memory.

"As these pictures will attest—and we can certainly add witness testimony as well—with the exception of providing advice to Coast Eagle airlines in order to save passenger lives, Mr. Henderson has spent virtually every day with his half brother since arriving in Atlanta."

"Objection," Roth's lawyer repeated. "This isn't a contest to see who can rack up more baby hours."

Destiny countered, "This hearing is to establish who is the most appropriate guardian for Zachary. Time spent with the baby is absolutely relevant to that question."

"Ms. Welsley has obviously inappropriately used her temporary guardianship over Zachary to undermine my client's—"

"Ms. Welsley's conduct is not at issue."

Cole came to his feet. "May I speak, Your Honor?"

The gallery's attention swung to Cole, and both lawyers turned, as well.

The judge considered the question for a long moment.

"Yes," he said. "I think it would be valuable to hear from Mr. Henderson."

Destiny withdrew toward the plaintiff's table, clearly yielding the floor to Cole.

Zachary was quiet on Cole's shoulder, gently fingering his gray-and-red tie.

Cole took a deep breath before beginning. "To be perfectly candid, I have to say that when I read Samuel Henderson had died, I wasn't sorry. I didn't feel much of anything. All I knew about the man was that he'd broken my mother's heart. At that point, I wanted nothing to do with any of the Hendersons."

Cole shifted a couple of steps sideways to come out from behind the table. "As I've already stated, I didn't know about the will. And even if I had, I wouldn't have cared about it. I have a growing, thriving business of my own."

He absently rubbed Zachary's back. "When I finally did come to Atlanta, it was incognito and with the sole purpose of ensuring Zachary would be properly cared for. But from the first moment I met him, my brother insisted I pay attention to him."

Cole smiled fondly down at Zachary. "I don't know whether it was the sound of my voice, the smell of my skin or that I looked something like our father. But from that point on, this little guy has done everything in his power to tell me that he needs me, that it's my responsibility to take care of him, to protect him and to love him. He may not be able to talk, but he's made his desire clear."

Amber's chest went tight, and her throat closed over.

There was a catch in Cole's voice. "And he is right. He's so very right. No matter what you decide here today, Your Honor, Zachary is my brother. He will always be my brother. He will always need me, and I will always be responsible for his welfare. Not because I have to be, or should be, but because I love him, and I will fight with every breath in my body to keep him safe."

Cole went silent. If a pin had dropped in the courtroom, it would have echoed.

He stood a moment longer, then he sat down and placed a kiss on the top of Zachary's head.

Zachary tipped his chin and grinned up at him, gently patting the side of Cole's cheek. "Gak baw. Gak. Gak."

Amber nearly burst into tears.

"I agree, partner," Cole whispered softly. "I agree."

Everybody looked to the judge.

Even Roth's lawyer seemed dazed.

Destiny put her hand on Cole's shoulder.

The judge cleared his throat. "I find…" He paused, adjusting his collar, then rearranging a few sheets of paper in front of him.

He glanced to the bath picture that was still up on the screen. "This is a very unique situation. And I recognize that there is a lot of money at stake. I understand that Coast Eagle Airlines needs to be run effectively. And I understand that guardianship of Zachary Henderson is pivotal to the operation of the company and therefore to the safety and livelihood of thousands of employees and passengers."

Destiny's hand tightened on Cole's shoulder.

He turned to glance at Amber, and the worried expression on his face made her stomach sink. She blinked against tears all over again.

"However," said the judge, "the purpose of this hearing is to determine the best guardian for Zachary Henderson. I cannot let any of the complicating factors impact his well-being and his future." He lifted the gavel. "Therefore, I find in favor of the plaintiff. I grant full and permanent guardianship of Zachary Henderson to Cole Henderson." The gavel came down.

Amber didn't hear a thing as she burst from her seat at the same time Cole turned to face her.

She rushed through the little gate and flung her arms around both of them, her heart overflowing with gratitude.

Cole chuckled as he held her tight. "I can't believe you did it."

"Did what?"

"Turned Zachary into a puppy."

She pulled back and grinned. "I was so scared. But he went straight to you."

"You're a genius."

"It was a big risk."

"It worked."

"Well done, you two," Destiny chimed in, clapping one hand on each of them.

"Well done, you," said Amber in return. "You were brilliant."

"That was a great idea."

"So was using the pictures on my phone."

Roth marched past them, stone-faced, staring straight ahead.

Cole watched his back for a few seconds. "It's going to be an interesting day at the office tomorrow."

"I'm going to worry about *that* tomorrow," said Amber.

Cole gave her a nod. "Agreed. Tonight, we celebrate." A trace of concern seemed to flit through his eyes. "Tomorrow, we figure out the rest."

Thirteen

Cole set the champagne bottle on the fireplace hearth, handing one flute of champagne to Amber and taking the other for himself. "It's very convenient to have a well-stocked wine cellar."

"It is. And I finally managed to figure out the code," said Amber.

She was sitting beside him on the thick carpet, leaning back against the sofa. Zachary was fast asleep in bed, Otis on guard in the hallway outside his door, and the lights were dimmed throughout the penthouse. The flickering gas fire blended with the tiny white lights of the Christmas tree.

"Some of the wine is locked up?" Cole asked.

"I mean the color code to the price and vintage."

"Yeah?"

She raised her glass. "Oh, yes. We are enjoying a very fine vintage."

He didn't have the heart to tell her that champagne all tasted the same to him. "We have a lot to celebrate."

"You were brilliant."

"No, you were brilliant. I just picked up the ball."

"And carried it across the goal line."

"You threw the hail Mary pass."

She grinned. "I did, didn't I? To us, then, and our mutual brilliance."

"Don't forget about Zachary." If they'd scripted the event, the kid couldn't have pulled it off any better.

"He was perfect." She took a sip. "Oh, this is a good one."

Cole followed suit. It tasted like sweet, bubbly wine to him. "It is."

"I guess you're the chair of the board now," she said, stretching her arms out as she leaned back.

Cole felt an uncomfortable pull in his gut. "We should talk about something else."

"Did you see the look on Roth's face? He is both furious and terrified."

"I don't see him at Coast Eagle for the long term."

"Are you going to fire him right away?"

Cole took a swig of the champagne, wishing it was something stronger and less sweet. "That's a complicated decision."

And it wasn't a decision he was in a position to make. He'd have to be willing to stay at Coast Eagle for weeks, maybe months before he could figure out the quagmire of the company's inner workings. Not that he held out hope for Roth, but a knee-jerk reaction wasn't in the best interest of the company.

"You'll have to hire a president. Max is anxious to get back to the legal department."

Cole finished the glass and set it aside, fighting an urge to grab Zachary and drag Amber with them to the Alaskan border. Nobody else mattered.

"Can we talk shop tomorrow instead?" he asked, easing over beside her. "You look beautiful in the firelight."

Her blue eyes softened. "You think?"

"I know." He touched his finger to the bottom of her chin, lifting it ever so slightly to give her a kiss.

The champagne tasted a lot better on her than it had in the glass.

"Thank you, Cole," she whispered against his lips.

He scooted closer still and framed her face with his hands. "I'd do anything for you."

Her smile was beautiful. She was beautiful. She was smart and strong and capable. And she was the sexiest woman he'd ever laid eyes on.

He kissed her.

Then he kissed her deeper, longing radiating through him, pushing everything out of his mind, everything but Amber and how much he needed her.

When he came up for air, he reached for her glass, setting

it aside. Then he lay back, easing her on top of him, loving the press of her soft body against his. He ran his hands along her back, down to her thighs, remembering the exquisiteness of her form.

He slipped his hand beneath her shirt, touching the hot, supple skin of her back, stroking his palms upward.

"You're distracting me," she told him.

"That's the idea."

"We have to talk."

"I know."

"There are a thousand decisions to make."

"Not tonight."

"But—"

"Shh. Give me tonight." He could hear a note of desperation in his own voice. "The world will come apart soon enough."

"It won't be that bad."

But Cole knew it would. It was going to get very, very bad. He was Aviation 58, and she was Coast Eagle. And now he had Zachary.

When his office door burst open, Cole looked sharply up from his desk. He wasn't a stickler for protocol, but the action seemed rudely abrupt.

Then he saw that it was Roth.

He set down his pen and sat back in his chair.

Roth advanced into the room. "I *want* an explanation."

"Of what?"

The only unexpected thing Cole had done so far was to *not* fire Roth. And that was only because he wanted to leave that option for whoever became the next president. And he doubted Roth would demand an explanation for keeping his job.

"You were talking to Kevin Kent," Roth announced.

Cole was forced to hide his shock. Only Luca and Bartholomew had known about this morning's call. He couldn't imagine either of them telling Roth.

He bought himself some time while he mentally calculated both the damage and his next move. "And?"

Roth braced his hands on Cole's desk, leaning forward. "And we both know what that means."

"Do we?" Cole asked. His tone was mild, but his brain was still scrambling.

"It means you're looking to sell. Are you going to liquidate your interest, Mr. Loving Half Brother? Do you care so little about the Coast Eagle legacy that you'd sell it off, maybe break it up, whatever it takes to free up the cash that kid got you?"

"Leave my office," said Cole.

"If you're holding a fire sale, the senior management team deserves an explanation."

Cole felt his blood pressure creep up. "The senior management team will deal with whatever the *owner* decides."

"So you're selling out and pocketing the windfall," Roth spat.

"Leave," Cole ordered.

"No regard for *anyone* or anything else?"

Cole heard a gasp.

He glanced past Roth to see Amber in the doorway. Her eyes were wide and her face was pale as she clung to the doorjamb.

He swore under his breath, even as he vaulted from his chair. She was quick to turn away, dashing down the hall toward the elevator.

He followed at a run. When he caught her, she was frantically stabbing the down button.

"Calm down," he told her in an undertone.

She didn't look at him. "Is it true?"

"I'm not having this conversation in the foyer."

In his peripheral vision, he caught the interested look of Sandra, the executive receptionist. He remembered how friendly she'd been with Roth the first day he'd visited. And it occurred to him that she had a phone number readout on her switchboard.

Amber turned, jaw clenched. "Just tell me if it's true."

"Come back to my office."

"Tell me the truth. Are you going to sell Coast Eagle?"

He scrambled for a way out of the conversation. "It's complicated. We need to talk. And we can't do it here."

She pressed her lips together, staring at him with disdain.

"Come back to my office, where it's private. You can hate me just as easily there."

She didn't answer.

"Amber," he prompted.

"Fine."

He turned and gestured for her to go first.

He let the distance grow between them. Then he stopped at Sandra's desk. He pinned the woman with a furious glare. "If you *ever* research my phone calls again and report them to *anyone,* I'll fire you on the spot."

The color drained from her face.

Leaving, he followed Amber into his office.

She was standing at the window, back to him, staring into the sunny Atlanta afternoon.

He closed the door, composing and discarding opening lines. "I was going to talk to you tonight."

She turned. "I can't believe I fell for it—hook, line and sinker."

He automatically moved toward her. "You didn't fall for anything. I've barely decided. I only decided this morning that selling is the best thing for everyone."

"You mean the best thing for you."

"No, not for me." He amended that statement. "Yes, okay, for me. But only because I could never do it. It's not humanly possible to run two airlines. I wanted to do it. I thought about doing it. Believe me, I came at doing just that from every angle I could."

"Over an entire two days?" she taunted.

"And before."

"Before? You'd planned to sell out *before* we even went to court?"

"I didn't *plan* to sell out. I considered the possibility that I might *have* to sell out."

"You don't *have* to do anything, Cole."

He hated the coldness in her eyes. "I have a plan."

"Clearly, you've had a plan all along. Do you have a conscience? Do you have a soul?"

"A plan for us," he explained. "I want you to come to Alaska as often as you can."

She reached out to grip the window ledge. Her voice was a rasp. "Alaska?"

"To see Zachary. And me, of course." He hoped she'd want to see him. She had to want to see him. He'd come to need her in his life.

She scoffed. "Last time you invited me to Alaska, you admitted you were being insincere and misleading, even manipulative."

It took him a second to remember his words. But he did, and he regretted them deeply. "That was a long time ago."

"The truth is the truth, Cole. Like I said back then, you don't need to worry. I won't be dropping by Alaska to bother you."

"Will you hear me out?"

"I don't think so."

"For Zachary's sake, will you *please* hear me out?"

"Are you taking him away from me?"

"I'm taking him to Alaska, yes. But—"

"Then there's nothing more to say, is there?"

There was plenty more to say. But he could see that this was pointless. Maybe they could talk in a few days. Or maybe he should be patient and let things settle.

Zachary had to be his priority just then. And the Cambridge deal needed his immediate attention. He also needed to get back to Aviation 58. He couldn't stay away any longer.

He didn't want to wait to square this with Amber, but maybe it was for the best. She wasn't going to listen to him right now.

"I'm trying hard not to hurt you," he told her.

She moved for the door, her voice stone flat. "So nice that you at least tried."

* * *

Amber was never going to forgive Cole Henderson, and she'd probably never forgive herself. He and Zachary had been gone for nearly a week, and she'd rehashed every minute of the past month inside her head trying to figure out where she went wrong, and how she could have so thoroughly misjudged him.

"I should have realized," she told Destiny.

"Realized what?" Destiny was across the table from her at Bacharat's. It was Friday night, and the last thing Amber wanted to do was go back to the empty penthouse.

"I should have realized that with this much money at stake, all men would be ruthless."

Destiny toyed with her martini for a moment. She started to speak then stopped herself.

"What?" Amber asked.

"Don't shoot the messenger."

"Are you actually going to defend him?"

"No. But do you think maybe you should have heard him out?"

"Absolutely not." Of that, Amber was certain.

"Why?"

"Because he'd only make up more lies. You can't trust a liar."

"To be fair, you don't *know* he was lying."

Amber's voice rose. "I thought you said you weren't going to defend him."

"I'm not defending him."

"The man had a billion-dollar deal lined up less than forty-eight hours after he won the court case. You don't think that required a little preplanning?"

Destiny didn't seem to have an answer for that.

"I hate to say this," Amber continued, and she really did, "but Roth's right when he says it all looks suspicious."

Destiny paused a beat before responding. "Does it bother you that you're siding with Roth?"

It did bother Amber. But, bottom line, Cole had breezed into town for three short weeks, romanced her, then left with her nephew and a billion dollars.

"I made a huge mistake," she said, swallowing. "What if I never see Zachary again?"

"That's simply not going to happen," said Destiny.

"He's in *Alaska*."

"You can go to Alaska."

Amber shook her head. "No. No, I can't."

Destiny stared hard. "You can. You *will*. Not tomorrow and not next week, but you *will* go see Zachary."

"I'm mortified that I fell for Cole's act."

"I've known you for five years. You are not going to let your embarrassment get in the way of doing the right thing for your nephew."

"You sound like you have faith in me." Amber wasn't sure she deserved anybody's faith.

"I have nothing *but* faith in you."

"Thanks." Amber polished off her martini, trying to feel some faith in herself. "I think I need another."

"I'm with you." Destiny signaled for another round. "Luca has been texting all day."

"I'm sorry it went bad with Luca."

"It didn't go bad with Luca." Destiny's tone was a little sharp.

"I didn't mean—"

"It was too *short* with Luca." Destiny's tone mellowed. "But it was all good. I really do miss him."

"I don't miss Cole."

"That's a big fat lie. You might be ticked off at him, but you have to miss him."

"I'm—"

Destiny spoke overtop her. "This sharing-our-feelings thing isn't going to work if you're just going to lie to me."

Amber tried to wrap her head around the jumble of her feelings for Cole. "I can't miss a man who didn't exist."

"Tell me something," said Destiny, propping her elbow on the tabletop and her chin on her hand. "If Cole was real, if the guy you met was authentic, would you be in love with him right now?"

"That's a pointless question."

"I saw you at the courthouse," said Destiny. "How you looked at him. How he looked at you. In that moment, you were a goner."

Amber remembered. And she experienced the feelings all over again—the intense rush of pride and respect for his strength and honesty, the knowledge that Roth had been vanquished and Zachary was safe, the certainty that she didn't have to worry anymore, that somebody else would help shoulder the burden, and the way he'd immediately turned toward her, the emotion in his eyes, her absolute certainty that nobody else in his world mattered, just her and Zachary.

"Amber?" Destiny prompted.

"Yes," Amber admitted. There really was no reason to lie to Destiny. "If that guy, the guy from the courtroom... If that guy truly existed, I'd be a goner."

Destiny's phone chimed. She looked at the number display and then put the phone to her ear. "Destiny Frost."

She listened for a moment, and her eyes narrowed.

Amber selfishly hoped that whatever it was wouldn't drag Destiny away tonight.

"What kind of paperwork?" asked Destiny. She sent a puzzled glance Amber's way.

Amber frowned.

"Is there a rush?" asked Destiny. "I've had a couple of martinis."

Amber couldn't help feeling disappointed. She didn't want Destiny to leave.

"We're at Bacharat's."

We? Amber glanced around the room, looking to see if she recognized anyone else from Destiny's firm. She didn't.

"Sure," said Destiny. "We'll be here."

As Destiny ended the call, Amber gathered her purse.

"What are you doing?" asked Destiny.

"Getting out of your way." Amber started to rise.

"Well, don't. That was about you."

Amber sat back down. "What about me? Am I being fired already?"

"No. Good grief, where did that come from?"

"Roth's still a VP."

"And Cole still owns the company."

"Only until the deal is finalized."

"Don't be paranoid. You're good at your job, and the new guys are going to see that. And this has nothing to do with your job." Destiny grinned.

"So who was that?" asked Amber.

"Fredrick Galloway of Galloway, Turner and Hopple."

"That means nothing to me."

"He's Cole's new Atlanta lawyer."

A wave of apprehension washed over Amber. "What does he want?"

"He was pretty cagey. Galloway's the top attorney at the top firm in the city."

"I'm sure Cole can afford the best." Though she didn't need it, Amber took another sip of her martini.

"He's got some kind of paperwork for you."

"I don't know what more I can give him. I've already given him—" Amber suddenly teared up. "Oh, damn."

Destiny reached for her hand. "It's going to be fine."

Amber looked into her friend's eyes. "Why did I go and fall in love with him?"

"I wish I could—"

"Ms. Frost?"

Amber looked up to see a sixtyish, fit, well-groomed man standing next to their table.

Destiny came to her feet, purely professional and polite. "Mr. Galloway. It's a pleasure to meet you."

Amber managed a smile.

"I'm sorry to interrupt your evening," said Mr. Galloway. "And, please, call me Fredrick."

"This is my client, Amber Welsley."

"Ms. Welsley." He gave her a nod.

"Amber," she automatically corrected.

Fredrick looked around. "Reception was able to provide us with a private meeting room on the fourth floor. Would you mind joining me there?"

"We'd be happy to," Destiny answered.

Amber took her purse and her coat, doing a double check behind her to make sure she hadn't left anything on the table.

They made their way to the reception elevator, going up one floor to the club's meeting rooms. Fredrick led them down a quiet hallway to a large boardroom. The lights had been turned on and coffee set out on a side table.

Destiny poured herself a cup, but Amber decided to let her stomach rest for a bit.

Fredrick took a seat near the end of a long table. Destiny and Amber sat across from him.

"As I said on the phone," he opened, "you're welcome to take the package with you to read over the weekend. I'd appreciate it if we could talk again Monday morning."

"We can make that happen," said Destiny.

Amber slid a sideways glance at Destiny, gauging her reaction. She seemed impressed by the man, and not overly concerned about the paperwork.

"In a nutshell," Fredrick continued, "Cole Henderson is setting up a trust fund for Zachary."

Amber couldn't hold her tongue. "How incredibly magnanimous of him."

Fredrick gave her a surprised look.

Destiny grabbed her knee under the table.

"What?" Amber looked at them both. "He steals a billion dollars from Zachary, and now he wants to set up a trust fund? What is it, for college or something?"

She wasn't clear on what it had to do with her. Maybe Cole wanted her to believe he was taking care of Zachary so she wouldn't go gunning for him.

Wasn't that a rule of a good con? Make sure the mark's not too angry with you when you leave? She was sure she'd seen that in a movie somewhere.

Fredrick cleared his throat. "My client has requested that Ms. Welsley, Amber, be named trustee with full power to make all decisions regarding the trust fund until Zachary Henderson reaches the age of eighteen."

"Sure," said Amber with a careless shrug. "I'll make sure he gets to college."

This time, Fredrick seemed to be fighting a smile. He slid a sheaf of papers across the table to Destiny. "The trust fund will also provide a salary for Amber."

"I'm not taking any of the money for myself," Amber scoffed. "Just because certain other people believe it is perfectly acceptable to—"

"Amber," Destiny interrupted.

"—use a defenseless baby as a means to—"

"Amber!"

Amber snapped her mouth shut. "What?"

"It says all proceeds from the sale of Coast Eagle Airlines."

The words didn't mean anything to Amber.

Destiny spoke slowly, articulating each word. "*All* the proceeds from the sale of Coast Eagle go into the trust for Zachary."

Amber cocked her head sideways, struggling to make sense of Destiny's words. "I'm not following."

"Cole is putting the whole billion into a trust fund for Zachary."

"Dollars?" Amber asked in a dry whisper.

"To be managed by you, as accountant, and he's suggested me as legal counsel, but you have discretion over that." Destiny sent a glance to Fredrick.

Fredrick nodded his confirmation.

Destiny continued, "Until Zachary is eighteen, at which time an orderly and gradual dispersal will begin to move control to Zachary."

Amber swiped her hair back from her forehead. "I know I'm

a little tired. But I thought you just said Cole put me in charge of *all* of the money."

"He did," said Destiny, a grin nearly splitting her face.

"And unlimited trips to Alaska," said Fredrick. He leaned forward and pointed to a spot on the page. "You get an annual salary, benefits and he was *very* specific about the unlimited trips to Alaska."

Amber instantly woke up. Her mind flashed back to the fight they'd had in Cole's office. *I have a plan,* he'd said. *A plan for us. I want you to come to Alaska as often as possible.*

Her hand flew to her mouth. "Oh, no."

"This is good," said Destiny. "This is amazing. I'm…" She looked helplessly to Fredrick.

"Mr. Henderson's instructions are clear and specific," said Fredrick. "And Galloway, Turner and Hopple is pleased to be working with you. This file will have my personal attention."

"He wasn't a fraud," said Amber, as much to herself as to Destiny.

Cole wasn't a fraud, and that meant Amber was in love with him. And she'd made a horrible mistake.

Cole now knew where he'd gone wrong. He never should have left Amber in Atlanta. And he should have brought her in on the decisions around Zachary from the very beginning. He knew she'd seen the trust fund documents; Fredrick confirmed he'd delivered them Friday night.

Cole had expected to hear from her. He'd expected her to understand his logic and like his solution. But it was Monday morning and there hadn't been a single word. Luca had called Destiny, but even she didn't respond.

It was late last night when he'd had the epiphany. Amber didn't want to be brought in at the end of the discussion. She wanted, needed and deserved to be a part of any decision involving Zachary. She also needed to be part of any decision involving Cole.

He knew he was in love with her, completely and forever.

That meant they'd be partners, completely and forever. So long as he could convince her to forgive him.

He wheeled his SUV into the terminal parking lot at the Juneau airport and turned to Zachary strapped into the car seat behind him.

"Got another trip in you?" he asked.

"Gak," said Zachary.

Cole grinned. "I'm going to take that as a yes."

He extracted Zachary, opened the hatchback to retrieve the small duffel bag he'd thrown together this morning. They were catching a scheduled flight, a big, fast jetliner that would get them to Seattle and then Atlanta as quickly as possible.

He balanced Zachary on one hip and lifted the duffel bag with his other hand, elbowing the hatchback closed. "Let's go get her, buddy."

It was a short walk to the main terminal entrance.

Cole would normally just hop in the back of the plane, not particularly caring about amenities. But with Zachary in tow, he'd gone with a first-class ticket. He'd been up most of the night figuring out his problems, and he hoped both of them could sleep for a few hours on the way.

He crossed the lobby toward the check-in lineups.

"Cole?" came a soft, familiar voice.

He stopped dead, not believing it could be true.

But when he turned, there she was, less than five feet away. She was smiling and her blue eyes shone. His heart lurched in his chest.

"Amber." He was in front of her in two strides, dropping the duffel bag to the floor.

"I was coming to see you," she told him.

Zachary immediately lunged for her. She caught him and pulled him to her chest.

"I was coming to you," said Cole. "I was so wrong. I'm so sorry."

Zachary patted her cheek, and she laughed.

"I'm the one who is sorry." She sobered as she told Cole, "I never should have doubted you."

"You had plenty of reasons to doubt me. I hoped you'd understand when you got the trust fund."

"I did understand. That's why I'm here." She gave a little laugh. "Well, that, and it was included in my salary package."

"I was wrong," Cole repeated.

Her expression faltered.

"About selling Coast Eagle," he quickly clarified. "That's not my decision to make alone."

She looked confused. "But you said you couldn't run them both."

"I know. And I can't. But I didn't explore all the options. I have now. And we have another option. But I'm not making this decision without you." He took a breath, steadying himself, realizing he was trying to tell her too much and all at once.

He stopped talking and drew her into his arms, her and Zachary, holding them both close.

"I love you," he whispered in her ear. "I love you so much. And I need you. And Zachary needs you. And you have to marry me. And you have to be his mother, because that's the only way this works. It's the only way he gets what he deserves out of life." He was talking too much again, but he couldn't stop himself. "You and I both had to compromise, but Zachary doesn't. He can have it all, Amber. But only if you'll marry me. I'm sorry. That was too much to throw at you. But once I started talking—"

"Yes," she said, drawing back. "Yes, I love you. And yes, I'll marry you. And of course, *yes,* I'll be Zachary's mother."

He kissed her deeply, until Zachary squirmed between them. "Gak!"

Cole chuckled, and Amber laughed as he drew back to give Zachary some space.

"Can you handle another thing?" he asked her.

"Things like you love me and want to marry me? Those kinds of things? Bring them on."

"We can merge the airlines."

She looked confused.

"But only if you want to do it. This is a decision we're making together. We can still do the trust fund instead. But Luca and I sat up all night last night. He's on board. We merge the airlines and run them together."

"Coast Eagle expands to Alaska?" she asked.

"No." Cole shook his head. "Aviation 58 expands to Atlanta. The head office stays here, but we live in both places."

"Yes," she said again. "Oh, yes."

"Can you handle one more?" Cole asked, feeling as if he was on a roll.

"*There* you are!" Destiny appeared out of the throng. "Hey, Cole. How did you know we were coming in on this flight?"

"I didn't," said Cole. "I was heading for Atlanta."

Destiny grinned at that. She turned to Amber. "I told you so. Did I not tell you so?"

"You did," Amber agreed with a smile.

"Hey, Zachary," Destiny greeted him.

"Does Luca know you're here?" asked Cole.

"I just called him."

Cole glanced at his watch. "Then, I expect he'll be here in about two minutes."

The Aviation 58 offices were on the far side of the airport grounds, but Cole knew Luca wouldn't waste any time getting to Destiny.

"So how're you two doing?" asked Destiny, jiggling Zachary's little hand.

"He's not selling Coast Eagle," said Amber.

Destiny froze, looking worriedly at Amber. "So you're out of a job?"

"She just agreed to marry me," said Cole.

"I was gone maybe five minutes," said Destiny.

"I work fast," said Cole. "We're going to run it together, as a family."

Luca appeared at a run, laughing as he scooped Destiny into

the air, kissing her hard and twirling her around. "I hope you don't plan to leave anytime soon."

Cole drew Amber close again. "You're not leaving, *ever*."

Fine by her. "I'm staying right here."

"I love you *so* much."

Zachary reached for Cole, and he lifted him from Amber's arms, settling him once more on his hip. Then he looped his arm around Amber's shoulder, realizing in a rush of happiness that he had a family. He had a perfect little family of his very own.

"That last thing?" he whispered into her ear.

"Yes?"

"Brothers and sisters for Zachary?"

"Just as soon as you're ready."

Cole was ready now.

* * * * *

If you loved THE MISSING HEIR,
pick up these other stories
from USA TODAY bestselling author
Barbara Dunlop

REUNITED WITH THE LASSITER BRIDE
THE LAST COWBOY STANDING
A COWBOY'S TEMPTATION
MILLIONAIRE IN A STETSON
A CONFLICT OF INTEREST

Available now from Harlequin Desire!